Secrets of Selkie Bay

Secrets of Selkie Bay

Shelley Moore Thomas

WITHDRAWN

FARRAR STRAUS GIROUX/NEW YORK

Farrar Straus Giroux Books for Young Readers
175 Fifth Avenue, New York 10010

Printed in the United States of America by
R. R. Donnelley & Sons Company, Harrisonburg, Virginia
First edition, 2015
1 3 5 7 9 10 8 6 4 2

mackids.com

Library of Congress Cataloging-in-Publication Data

Thomas, Shelley Moore, author.
    Secrets of Selkie Bay / Shelley Moore Thomas. — First edition.
       pages cm
    Summary: Selkie Bay is a place where the old legends seem very near, and
eleven-year-old Cordelia believes that her secretive mother is a selkie who has
returned to the sea—a belief that offers some hope as she struggles to care
for her two younger sisters and help her scientist father make ends meet
in their home by the sea.
    ISBN 978-0-374-36749-7 (hardcover)
    ISBN 978-0-374-36750-3 (e-book)
    1. Selkies—Juvenile fiction.   2. Families—Ireland—Juvenile fiction.
3. Missing persons—Juvenile fiction.   4. Mothers and daughters—Juvenile
fiction.   5. Fathers and daughters—Juvenile fiction.   6. Seals (Animals)—
Juvenile fiction.   [1. Selkies—Fiction.   2. Family life—Ireland—Fiction.
3. Missing persons—Fiction.   4. Mothers and daughters—Fiction.
5. Fathers and daughters—Fiction.   6. Seals (Animals)—Fiction.
7. Ireland—Fiction.]   I. Title.

PZ7.T369453Sd 2015
813.54—dc23
[Fic]

2014040357

Farrar Straus Giroux Books for Young Readers may be purchased for business
or promotional use. For information on bulk purchases please contact
Macmillan Corporate and Premium Sales Department at (800) 221-7945 x5442
or by email at specialmarkets@macmillan.com.

To Noel, Isabelle, and Caledonia,
for the little bits and pieces I borrowed.

And to Susan, who taught me
what it means to be a sister.

Secrets of Selkie Bay

Numb

NUMB IS THAT FEELING YOU GET when you forget your mittens because it is late spring so the mittens are all put away, and the wind howls like a flock of banshees and the air is wet with spray and you have to take a note to your da at the bad end of the docks. You can't put your hands in your pockets because you have to push your baby sister in the pram. And your other sister doesn't help because, well, she just doesn't. And you have to take a note in the first place because your mum said to and besides, no one ever answers a phone at the bad end of the docks. That feeling in your fingers, the very tips, where it's cold, then hot, then nothing. That's numb.

Numb is also the feeling you get when you come home and your mum's gone and then your da has to tell you that he doesn't know when she's coming back. And if he knows why she left or where she went, he doesn't tell you because there just aren't that many words left anymore.

That's what numb feels like.

Letter in a Book

MUM HAD BEEN GONE for two months when I found the letter.

I don't know why I didn't notice the old book there before, sticking out of my bookshelf like a tall, thin soldier among its shorter, thicker companions. But there it was. So I pulled it out.

A *Child's Book of Selkies*—my mum's old folklore collection—was stuffed right between *Matilda* and *The Yellow Fairy Book*. I hadn't seen it in years. The cover was worn and frail, probably from all the times I'd asked Mum to read it to me, back when I believed in fairy stories. Back when I believed in magic and happily-ever-afters. But somewhere around the time Ione came along, the book had disappeared. I always figured Ione had shredded it up to make doll clothes, or buried it in the yard, pretending it was treasure, or maybe even eaten a page or two. Not that my eight-year-old sister would eat a book *now*, but as a baby, she ate a lot of paper.

Carefully, so the cover wouldn't crumble away, I opened it.

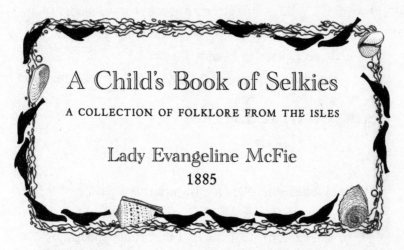

A Child's Book of Selkies

A COLLECTION OF FOLKLORE FROM THE ISLES

Lady Evangeline McFie
1885

Framing the title page was a border of intertwined seals, as well as long ropes of seaweed, and a sprinkling of pearls and shells. It looked incredibly old-fashioned and I remembered how much I loved it. I had named each of the seals around the edges, fifteen of them, but I couldn't even remember one of their names now.

And then there was the smell. Salt, seaweed, musty old paper. The scent reminded me of Mum, except for the musty part. I closed it gently and, not wanting to put it back on the shelf yet, carried it with me as I tidied the house. Someone had to pick up, since Da left his things everywhere—socks that were on the floor and never found the hamper, and waterfalls of blankets that trailed down the side of his unmade bed.

I was making his bed when the letter fell out of the book. The tight, scrolling, curved writing could only belong to my mum. My stomach clenched, like some invisible fist had just squeezed and twisted it. *Mum*.

I let the treasured, fragile *A Child's Book of Selkies* fall to the floor.

> *To my darling Cordie,*
>
> *I know you will find this, sooner or later, my reader girl. You couldn't stay away from this book when you were a tot. I wish I were brave enough to hand this note to you in person, but I have to do it this way. Someday you will understand.*
>
> *The first thing you must know is that I love your father with the same love that stars have for the night or that trees have for the rich soil that nourishes their roots. Had I been a star or a tree, I'd not be writing this letter, for I would still be there with your father.*
>
> *And with you.*
>
> *But I am not made of stardust nor sturdy bark. And sometimes one is not as strong as one wishes to be. And so I have to go. I am not certain how long I will be gone, but I will try to come back to you as soon as I can.*

While I am away, take care of your da. Don't
let him work too hard. Don't spend the money in
the sugar jar too quickly. Use what you need, but
try to make it last. And keep the Dreaming Lass
seaworthy. Don't let Ione and Neevy forget the
taste of salt spray on their tongues.

And please, Cordie, do not worry about me.
Watch over your sisters. Keep them safe.

"Whatcha got there?" Ione asked, trying to grab the
letter from my hand as she barged into my parents' room.
Since school had let out for the summer, Ione was forever
on my heels. There were no friends' houses I could send
her to, since Ione refused to step outside the door for very
long. She was convinced Mum would pop back home the
instant she left. Besides, neither of us had many friends
anymore. Kids are afraid when something bad happens
to you, like it is contagious or something. As if the fact
that my mum had gone would make every mum in town
disappear.

I didn't have much time for friends, anyway.

I held the letter up high so Ione couldn't reach. Not that
I really needed to hide the letter from her. She couldn't read
near as well as me. She claimed that words, when written
close and small, ran together in her mind like they were
dancing or playing a game upon the page.

Mum knew this. That's why she wrote the words so close and small, I think.

"Come on! Let me take a peek!" Ione begged, still trying to grab it. "Is it from a boy? You're too young to have a boyfriend, Cordie. Wait until Da hears about this!" Ione danced about the room with her usual grace. Everything Ione did was graceful, as if an invisible breeze held her up and controlled her moves. As if she were part of the air. "Cordie's got a boyfriend! Cordie's got a boyfriend!" she sang.

Even her teasing voice was pleasant, floating across our cottage on fairy wings. I wanted to slug her. But instead, I remained calm. It was best, when Ione got herself all wound up, to bring her back down to earth in a gentle way. Otherwise, she'd be singing songs about me and imaginary boys for the rest of the day.

"I don't have a boyfriend. Eleven-year-olds don't have boyfriends," I said simply, even though I was almost twelve. "It's just a . . . a note from the landlord. The rent will be due soon. Da will need to remember this time," I lied. Though the part about remembering to pay wasn't a lie. Since Mum left, Da had forgotten many things. I didn't want to think about the fact that we probably didn't have any money for the rent this month at all.

"Oh." Ione stopped her dancing. "Well, that's not very interesting, is it?"

"No, I'm afraid it isn't," I agreed. "Now, go and do something quiet before you wake the wee beast." I hoped she didn't see my hand shake as I folded the letter and put it in my pocket.

"Remember when she took long naps? Babies shouldn't be allowed to stop taking long naps. Hey, what's that old book on the floor?"

And as if she were psychic, our baby sister roused with a pterodactyl-like cry from her tiny room down the tinier hallway. I gave Ione the *it's your turn* look. She huffed off as I picked up the old book. The faded seal smiled at me from the cover.

For the first time in a long time, when I thought of Mum, I smiled.

And that's what hope feels like.

D*a*

"WHERE ARE MY GIRLS?" Da called when he got home an hour later. "Where are the Sullivan sisters?"

He took Neevy from my arms, gave each of us a hug, and snuggled our cheeks with his stubbly ones. He was always scruffy by the end of the day. Mum once said that if he put his mind to it, he could grow a beard by sundown. The sharp tang of the resin he used on the boats he repaired enveloped us all.

"Phew," Ione said, holding her nose. I didn't mind the smell.

Da hoisted Neevy in the air in front of his face and took a whiff. "Speaking of *phew*," he said, passing the baby off to Ione.

"I made your favorite for dinner," I said.

"Everything you make is my favorite, Cordie," Da said. "It's better than—" But he didn't finish. We all used to joke about Mum's cooking before she left, even Mum herself.

She made excellent shrimp-and-pesto pasta, and a lovely blackberry cobbler from the berries we picked outside our window, but the rest of her meals were not very tasty. A pained look crossed Da's face for an instant, then he lifted the lid of the pot on the stove.

"Mmm. Potato soup." He sniffed a big sniff, then lowered the lid and looked at me squarely. "Thank you, my dear."

We ate to the sound of spoons hitting bowls, and slurps, but no words.

After supper, I set Ione to washing up and I looked after little Neevy.

That was the saddest part of Mum leaving. Neevy was only ten months old now. After two months of Mum being gone, I bet Neevy didn't even remember her. At least Ione and I could still picture Mum in our minds, with her deep black hair that looked almost blue in the twilight, and her eyes, dark and large like onyx.

Ione has the look of Mum, hair and eyes and all. I have the eyes, too, but my hair is a dull copper, like Da's. As for Neevy, it's too early to tell, her head still being bald as an egg. Mum's boss at the hair salon, Maura, said not to worry until her first birthday, which was still a couple months off. But if no hair had appeared by then, well, that'd mean bad luck. Poor Neevy's bad luck came early, I guess, not having a mum around to watch over her and coax her little hairs to grow.

From the kitchen, I could hear the difference between Ione's splashing in the suds and Da's methodical scrubbing. We had a deal, Da and I. Whenever Ione washed the dishes, one of us would check and rewash what needed it. Ione never managed to scrub all the bits of food out of the bowls, especially if it was potato soup. And if the potato soup dried on the bowl, it would take more than the wire brushes Da used on his boats to pry it off. I waited for him to start whistling some old sailing tune he'd heard from the men at the dock, until I remembered he didn't whistle much anymore. I looked at Neevy, lying on her tum, kicking her legs and moving across the floor as if she were swimming on the carpet. She'd be fine for a minute. I went into the kitchen.

"Da?" I said, fingering Mum's letter in my pocket.

"Hmm?" He had finished with the bowls and was now carefully rinsing the goggles that protected his eyes from flying splinters and airborne fiberglass at work. Most of the men washed theirs at the docks, but Da always wanted to hurry home.

I searched for the words, but then I realized that I didn't know which ones I wanted. *Should I share the letter with him?*

I was quiet for a little too long.

"Cordie, is this about your mum?" He had turned off the water and was facing me now.

I nodded.

"You miss her, don't you?"

I nodded again.

"I miss her, too." That's what he always said when I tried to talk about her. *I miss her, too.*

And that was all.

I felt hotness in the back of my eyes. *Don't cry, Cordie. It will just make Da feel worse.* I blinked away the tears and then he was hugging me.

"Let's not talk about her right now, Cordie. I know it hurts too much."

I let myself cry only for a moment and I think Da was crying, too. Then I sniffed a big sniff. I tried to wipe the wetness of my tears from Da's shirt, but then realized it was already wet from the washing. I looked up at him, waiting for him to meet my eyes and tell me that it would be all right. But he didn't. He just went to that silent place inside of himself, and then he cleared his throat, turned to the sink, and finished his work.

"Good night, Cordie," he said when I finally left the kitchen.

Da was like a biscuit that had fallen to the floor and crumbled.

It would not be easy to put him back together.

Isle of Dreams

DA SAID WE COULD WATCH a show on television before bedtime, but we didn't really want to. That was something we used to do, all of us, together. We'd curl up on the couch and eat scrambled-egg sandwiches for dinner and watch nature shows about Tasmanian devils, endangered wolves, or migrating whale pods. Our favorites were always the ones about the sea. Otherwise, Mum and Da didn't like us watching much TV, not when there were books to read inside and mud pies to make outside. Back then, watching TV had been a treat. But tonight, as with every other night since Mum had been gone, neither Ione nor I had much desire to lay even one finger on the remote. It just felt wrong.

In our room that night, after Ione fell asleep, I crawled under the covers of my bed and switched on my flashlight. I read the letter over and over until my eyes felt dry and burning. I read until my stomach hurt from flopping around so much. One minute I'd find myself happy, thinking about her and hoping she'd be back soon—hadn't she said she'd *try to come back*? And the next minute I'd be mad, furious actually, that she had left in the first place. She said she had a reason, but really, what reason would ever be good enough to leave us? Eventually, I fell asleep with the letter squashed in my hand, dreaming of the last time Mum and I were out on our tiny motorboat, the *Dreaming Lass*.

Ione had been there, too. And Neevy. Mum had her strapped to the front of her in one of those little baby harnesses. The sky was swirling with low clouds, and old Archibald Doyle, with his white strings of hair dancing around his wrinkly head, had stood on the beach that morning, arms crossed, glaring.

"You think you'll see something out in that, do you?" he asked, motioning to where the clouds kissed the waves, with no actual sky in between.

"Stay out of my business, Mr. Doyle. I know what I am doing," Mum had cried over the top of the wind. I remember how Mr. Doyle shook his head in disgust and turned away from us, heading up the beach.

And then we were speeding along and the little motorboat was pitching. My stomach was lurching, as usual. Even in my dream, I felt the urge to throw up.

"Oh, Cordie, the sea is not so bad," Mum had said to me, taking the hand that wasn't steering the boat to smooth my hair from my damp face.

"I'm okay when it's flat, but when it rolls like this, I feel it in my guts."

"Why is your face so gray, Cordie?" Ione asked.

We bounced along the choppy waves until Mum cut the motor and said, "There. If you look *there*. Can you see it? Can you see the shimmer of it?"

We shook our heads. The mist was thickening even more. And the waves were getting higher. But then maybe, just over the tip of the foam, I saw a faint glimpse of . . . something.

"We must navigate in between those two huge rocks," Mum was saying, pointing to two dark forms in the otherwise white distance. "The black ones. They are ragged and dangerous. Many an experienced sailor has unwittingly thrust his boat upon their jagged edges." Leave it to Mum to make everything an adventure. "After we pass through, we can see it better, but we'll have to be careful."

"See what? Where are we going?" Ione's voice echoed in the wind as a patch of fog enveloped us, thick and cottony. "I can't see anything."

"Why, the magic island of the selkies, of course." Mum had used her teasing voice. The fog was too thick to make out her expression.

"Oooooh," Ione and I said together. *"The selkies."*

"Don't laugh," Mum said, but she was laughing, too.

"I thought you didn't like talking about the selkies," I said.

"I don't like the way people in this town talk about them,

the way they exploit the legend, and that's a different thing altogether," said Mum. The fog moved in clumps between us, surrounding us like a worn-out blanket.

"Aren't they just pretend, Mum?" Ione asked. "Are there really such things as selkies?"

Mum turned toward me. "What do you think, Cordie?" she asked. "You know the legends."

You couldn't live in a place called Selkie Bay and not know the legends. Half of the businesses on the main street had something to do with selkies. "Yes," I said. "I know them."

"Well, what do you think? Do you believe that shape-shifting selkies live on a secret island with rocky shores where they hide their magical seal coats?"

"I dunno," I said too quickly.

"Ah, well, then I don't know, either."

"I do!" Ione cried. "I believe in them!"

"Then let's go find that island!" Mum cried. She revved the motor and we were racing again, but the mist still twirled around us and I felt like I was spinning, spinning like a top.

After a few minutes, Mum looked around and sighed. "Oh well, can't see much of anything. Another day then. When I was a girl, I used to love that island—"

But she didn't finish her sentence because I had leaned over the side of the *Dreaming Lass*, and was now tossing my breakfast to the waves.

* * *

As I sat up in bed, the dream faded slowly. The rumpled letter had fallen from my hand. I reached down to the cold floor and felt around for it. I picked it up and smoothed it flat against my leg, then folded it as tiny as I could. I'd have to hide it in my clothes today so nobody would stumble upon it. By nobody, I meant Ione. She was such a snooper, and this note was between me and Mum.

The flashlight clattered to the floor, dim and lightless, having gone through the batteries during the night. No one heard the clank but me. Ione was snoring softly in her bed, and one room over, Da was snoring not so softly in his. Neevy gave the occasional slurp as she sucked on her fist in the tiny room just past Da's. Other than those comforting noises of the night, our small house was quiet, though I knew Da would be getting up for work soon.

I wouldn't have much time.

I crept about in the almost dark, the soft coming of daylight still only a promise, but it was light enough for me. I picked up *A Child's Book of Selkies* and gave it a quick scan. There were no telltale notes scrawled up the margins in Mum's handwriting. No clues whatsoever from this book about where a sugar jar full of money might be. And when had she started keeping money in the sugar jar, anyway?

When the jar had gone missing a couple of months back,

I first thought Ione had broken it and been too afraid to own up to it. When Ione told me angrily that she hadn't broken the sugar jar, and suggested that maybe the ants had run off with it, I thought perhaps Mum had taken it. Except that didn't make much sense. Da had been extra-quiet right after Mum disappeared. I didn't know what to say about anything, let alone a sugar jar that we couldn't find, so he and I never discussed it.

I padded through the narrow hallway, past the sitting room, and down the two stone steps to the kitchen. The old slab floor was freezing cold, as usual. It was the only room in the house that wasn't floored in creaky wood, and even when summer was at its hottest, it stayed cool. Ione and I often lay on our backs, arms stretched wide, soaking in the delicious chill before we went to bed. Mum would laugh, saying she didn't realize she had starfish for daughters as she gingerly stepped over us to get to the pantry. I, however, had no need for caution this morning, just silence. Tiptoeing, I crept ahead to the pantry and moved cans and jars around, this way and that. I could remember when the two shelves were stocked full. Now, I could easily see within seconds that they held no sugar jar.

Next, I checked all the cabinets and the refrigerator. As I opened the heavy white door, I wondered why I hadn't looked in the fridge first off. That was where I would hide money, if I had any. The light from the small bulb nearly blinded me, but after moving the almost-empty milk jug, a carton of eggs, a block of cheese, four small apples, and three nearly scraped-out jars of jam, I realized it wasn't there, either.

I crept to the hall, toward the room where Da lay snoring, then stopped. If she had put it in their room, Da would surely have found it by now, wouldn't he?

The coat closet in the hall was next.

I opened the door and it creaked a tiny bit. I found the string that hung from the ceiling and gave it a tug. With a click, everything was illuminated. The top shelf was empty. Leaning against one side of the closet was Neevy's fold-up pram. On the rack were several of Da's jackets and some of our sweaters that we hadn't needed since April. I touched the empty hanger where Mum's coat used to hang and it swung back and forth. It had been her special coat, sleek, smooth, and silvery black, but it was gone now. Only a bare spot remained.

The phone rang, making me jump back and bang my head against the closet door. I quickly shut it and ran to the phone, which sat in its usual spot on a blue-painted end table in the sitting room. As I always did, I imagined her voice on the other end and wondered what I'd say to her.

But Da got there first.

"Hello? Yes, this is Sullivan. Yes, I know I'm late with the payment. Next week. I'll pay it next week." Da hung up without a goodbye.

"The phone wake you up, too?" he asked.

I nodded.

"You'd think they'd wait until the sun came up. Greedy creditors." He went to the kitchen to heat some water for tea. "Well, since I'm already awake, I'm staying up. How about you?"

I nodded and got some mugs from the same cupboard I'd been searching through only moments ago.

"Da, have you seen the sugar jar?"

There was a pause. "I don't like sugar in my tea, Cordie. You know that."

"Yes, but I was just wondering—"

"If we are out of sugar, I can give you a little money to take to the store, but buy only a small amount." He handed me a few bills before I could say that I didn't really need the sugar, just the jar.

"Da—"

"I've got to go in early today, Cordie. Just get what you need in town. But don't be gone long. And make Ione go with you. It would be good for her to leave the house for a change."

The Mermaid's Tresses

WHEN DA WAS OFF TO WORK, I searched every nook and cranny in our little house for an hour. The jar was nowhere to be found. We needed that money.

I know I'm late with the payment . . . I'll pay it next week.

Exasperated, I went to check on Neevy. She had pulled herself up to the railing of her crib and was standing with her arms outstretched to me.

"Mmmmmuummmaaa," she cried.

These were the times my heart broke.

"No, sweet girl, it's just Cordie." Neevy snuggled against me and stuffed her plump thumb into her mouth. "Ione!" I called. "Can you get Neevy ready to go?"

There was no need to yell, but I did, anyway. Our house was tiny enough that if you stood in the kitchen in just the right place, you could see down the hall into each of the other small rooms of our house. The sitting room, the bathroom, and the bedrooms—mine and Ione's, Da's, and little Neevy's at the end.

Ione stumbled sleepily down the short hallway and stopped in front of me with a gigantic yawn.

"We are going to town," I said.

"Where in town?"

"To . . . um . . . to the Mermaid's Tresses."

"Why do we need to go there?" Ione put one hand on her hip in her stubborn pose. She used to love going to the salon, hanging out on the swivel chairs, talking to Maura and Mum just like she worked there herself.

"We just do."

"What if Mum comes home while I'm gone?" Ione's big dark eyes got glassy and it looked like a tear was forming in the left one. If she started crying, then I'd probably start, too. And it wouldn't take much to get Neevy going as well.

There was no time for crying today, not if I was going to make us some money.

"Yeah, well, we are going, Ione. Hurry up and get ready. And get the pram," I said in my most businesslike voice. If I kept Ione moving and busy, maybe I could avoid a scene. And maybe I could stuff my own worries back inside my heart and keep them there a while longer.

"You're not the boss of me. You're not . . ." Ione didn't finish. The unspoken words hung between us, like the only strand left of a broken spiderweb, dangling. I didn't have time for this. I didn't have time to mend the threads. I needed to get us to the Mermaid's Tresses, fast. The sooner Maura gave us jobs sweeping hair off the floors, the sooner we'd have money.

At this point, every little bit would help.

"I know, I know," I said delicately. "I'm not the boss of you. But we're both the boss of Neevy. So we better get this baby moving before she starts thinking she's queen of the world or something." It was like a dance sometimes, stepping carefully on the tips of my toes to keep Ione from starting a rage. I swung Neevy around, and she gave a deep baby chuckle. "See, she already thinks she's the queen of the world!"

I could see the emotions waging a battle right across Ione's face. Her eyes were narrowed, her nose was crinkled, but her mouth could not keep its frown. She *wanted* to be mad and she *wanted* to cry, but baby laughter is hard to resist.

"Queen of the world!" Ione repeated at last, taking Neevy from me and blowing on her belly to make her laugh harder. She swung her around and around, both of them giggling helplessly.

Moodiness avoided. For now.

In ten minutes, Ione was dressed and came wheeling around the corner, baby on her hip, having retrieved Neevy's collapsible pram from the closet. She unceremoniously dumped our sister in and buckled the strap. "Let's be quick about this."

We didn't lock the door, for Ione's sake. She liked the idea of leaving the door unlocked for Mum, in case she'd forgotten her keys. Besides, nobody really locked their doors in Selkie Bay. It was a safe town, even during the tourist season. Now, if we lived farther down the coast where the water was clearer, the days warmer, and the sand softer, then we might have worries. But the coldish waters of Selkie Bay didn't attract the bad element. Da had always said as much.

We set out for downtown Selkie Bay, a good twenty-minute walk from home, if you walked fast, which I did. Ione fairly ran next to me. We passed the three pubs in the town square, the Sea Queen's Treasure, Grania's Pieces of Eight, and Grace the Bald's—all named after the legendary pirate Grace O'Malley. Hundreds of years ago, a ship from her fleet sank off the coast of the bay, filled with gold. They found the wreckage, but they never found the treasure. Not ever. Makes you wonder if there ever really was a treasure. That's the way it is with legends around here. Lots of talk about things, but not much concern for what's true and what isn't.

We sped by the pubs, holding our noses since they reeked of yesterday's tobacco. And yesterday's beer as well. The stink was awful.

We were out of breath when we got to the Mermaid's Tresses, the front of which was painted aqua with rich chestnut trim. Years ago, someone had carved a giant likeness of a mermaid with flowing hair from golden beech wood. The wooden sculpture now adorned the front of the salon. It gave the shop a magical quality, like you were about to enter a salon for enchanted princesses instead of the regular old hairstyling place that it was.

The front door was propped open with a brick. Maura saw us right away. She left a customer mid-snip and gathered Ione and me into a big hug. She smelled of the salon's signature seaweed-and-mint shampoo and her soft arms reminded me for a minute of Mum's, except Mum's weren't wrinkled or floppy.

"Oh, hello, my luvs," Maura said. Then, handing me her shears, she unbuckled Neevy and picked her up for a snuggle. "Getting bigger every day. Still no hair." Maura planted a kiss on Neevy's cheek and gave her a biscuit from the jar on the counter. "Help yourselves," she said to Ione and me. Ione grabbed extras and stuffed them in her pockets. She knew Maura wouldn't mind. We had little money for fine treats like the ones in Maura's jar.

"You'll know Rose Sullivan's girls, don't you, Mrs. Gallagher?"

Mrs. Gallagher sat in the customer chair, with her wet, steel-gray hair dripping about her ears. She nodded, but didn't look us in the eye. That's what most folks did when they saw us, looked down or maybe off in another direction like there was something out there real important to see. *Poor Rose Sullivan's girls.*

"Rose was the one with the magic fingers." Maura winked at us and smiled.

Mrs. Gallagher's wet head bobbed again as she continued to study the linoleum.

"Alas, poor dearie," she said under her breath.

"Um, Maura," I said, playing with the chocolate biscuit. I was too nervous to eat it. "I was thinking maybe you could use some help, you know, sweeping up hair and the like."

"Me too. I'll help, too," said Ione. "If it's not for too long. I can't be gone from my house for too long, you know."

Already Ione was getting antsy, shifting her weight from one side to the next like she had to use the bathroom, and we'd just arrived.

"I'm afraid I'll be closing up day after tomorrow. My sister is ill and I've got to move her down from Oringford before the height of the tourist season. August gets crazy around here, you know—and it's only two weeks away! So no appointments for the rest of July."

My heart fell to my stomach. My whole reason for coming to the salon today was crashing to the ground.

"The Mermaid's Tresses won't be open for the rest of the month? Not at all?" I asked.

Maura shook her head. "Sorry, dears, but I can't leave my sister hanging when she needs me."

My face felt warm. The money I had imagined flew away, out the window, like lonely birds.

"I wish I had the money to keep it open while I am gone, but I'm afraid I don't. Look around, Cordelia. It's only the locals needing cuts right now, and they can wait a bit if need be. But when folks come in from the cities for their holiday, they'll want to get spiffed up and I'll need to be ready. I make enough from August through October to keep myself nice and cozy all winter. Really hoping it's a strong season this year—with lots of selkie sightings!" Maura laughed and rolled her eyes a little. "But it's just not like it used to be. Check with me when I get back, luvs. I'll find something for you girls to do then. Sure and I will."

I made my mouth smile, but I didn't really feel it in the rest of my face. Sweeping floors weeks from now wouldn't put money in our pockets today.

"Maybe you could try some of the other places here on the strip. I'm sure someone needs a hand." Maura turned her attention back to the sheep-like head of Mrs. Gallagher.

"I don't want to work in one of those dumb stores," whispered Ione to me as we walked over to the other side of the salon. "They'd probably make me clean the loo." She plopped herself down in the second chair from the left, Mum's old chair.

"I don't want to, either," I whispered, picking up Neevy and sitting with her on the floor. She played with my hand as she started to doze in my lap. "But I don't know if we have much choice. Da could use the money."

Ione hadn't heard the phone call this morning. She hadn't heard the strain in Da's voice. But I had.

"Ione, maybe if we—" I said. But she wasn't looking at me. She was looking at the empty sink, the one that Mum always used.

I glanced at the sink, then back at Ione, whose eyes were getting glassier by the second. The note from Mum was burning a hole in my pocket. I really wanted to tell Ione about it—but it said I needed to look after Ione, and that meant *not* worrying her.

"We'll take turns," I said. "If we get a job, we'll split it."

Ione curled her lips into a snarl as only she could. She picked up one of the magazines on the table next to her. "What kind of a person wants to read about n . . . nail p-p-polish and *bras*? What's *bras*?" she asked, pronouncing the word like *brass*. Then she chucked the magazine across the table, where it slid and knocked other magazines off.

"Nice," I said. "Real nice, Ione. Pick those up so Maura doesn't have to." She was about to get herself all worked up and refuse, I could see it in the way she held her shoulders, but I managed to head it off. "And when you're done you can read *this*. It's not about *bras*. I promise."

Ione blushed and said, "Bras? Ewww." Then she quickly grabbed the book I held out for her.

I'd put *A Child's Book of Selkies* in Neevy's diaper bag before we left. I'd been keeping it close by since I found it in my room, though I'm not sure why. Ione gave it a thumb-through. "I remember this book. Mum used to read it to us. It's got too big of words, though."

"Do you want me to read you some of it?" I said, taking the book, holding it over the head of Neevy, who slept in my lap, and opening to a page near the beginning. "Look, there's a section on how to spot a selkie."

The first thing you must learn about Selkies is how to recognize them in the wild. Should you come across one in its Seal form, you will not be able to tell if it is a shape-shifter or not. It is impossible. However, if you see a person and wonder perhaps if it is really a Selkie in Human form, there are ways to tell, if you are a noticing type of person:

1. Eyes and hair as black as night.
2. Slight to moderate webbing between fingers and/or toes. (The flippers never quite completely shift away.)
3. Possession of a fine gray or silver-black coat or cloak.

A combination of all three must exist. In addition, do not fear if you happen to meet one of these creatures in your endeavors. They are said to be the most devoted of parents and are known for making good fish pots.

"Sounds a little like Mum," Ione said. "Except that this book is boring and Mum was never boring."

It did sound a little like Mum.

"Aw, come on, Ione. Mum loved this kind of thing, didn't she? Remember when she took us out in the *Dreaming Lass* looking for the selkies' isle?"

Ione was squirmy. I knew what was coming next.

"We've been gone too long."

I nodded. "Yes, we should go." There was still more to do while we were out. "Come on. We have to get some sugar."

The Streets of Selkie Bay

IONE TRIED TO CONVINCE ME we didn't need sugar.

"I'll just take some packets from the tea tray at Maura's. She won't care."

"We have to buy some, Da said so. And he didn't mean to just take someone else's."

"It's not like we use much, anyway. And when did you find the sugar jar? Is it empty? I haven't seen it in weeks."

No one has. No one but Mum.

We were quick, in and out of Flipper's Fast-Mart in a matter of minutes with a small bag of sugar.

"Let's go home now," said Ione, jiggling the pram to wake Neevy. "See, Neevy's awake and she's going to be hungry. Or she's going to cry. We should go home."

"No, Ione. We are not going home yet. Since we walked all the way here, we are going to see if any of these stores will give us a job."

She jiggled the pram more forcefully, but Neevy, bless her, slept through it. "You are not serious," Ione said.

But I was.

I led us farther down the main street of Selkie Bay. The wind had kicked up, making it chilly for a summer morning. The road widened and led to the harbor and to the tourist shops that lined the water like colorful jewels in a king's crown. Next to the bright aqua of the Mermaid's Tresses was the dazzling emerald green of Seal Biscuits, a bakery that had nothing to do with seals, but everything to do with the best chocolate cookies in the world. Those were the treats that Maura kept in the jar on the counter of her salon. Seal Biscuits had striped awnings that matched the green outer walls perfectly.

Next to the bakery was Whale of a Tale, a bookstore painted bright red, with characters from famous stories carved into the heavy wooden door. It was my favorite shop because the owner never seemed to notice if you just sat in a chair and read books but never bought any. And across from the bookshop was the giant orange smiley-seal sign of Chippy's Fish and Chips. Even though Ione feared sliding around on all the splattered oil she was certain covered the floor, we still had to go in and try.

"Can you imagine having to scrape up all that grease?" She groaned. "Gross."

Unfortunately, it was the same story from one business to

the next. Well, not the same story, exactly, but they started the same. *"Oh, Cordelia and Ione Sullivan. Haven't seen you around in a while. Oh, look at the baby. My, how she's grown! So sorry about your . . . well . . ."* (This was where their eyes shifted around, trying to find the right place to look, which was anywhere but at our faces; our shoes were popular locations.) *"What brings you in?"*

And I told them that I was looking for a job. Then Ione would say, *"I'm not cleaning the loo."*

Here's where the stories changed. Sometimes it was because their nieces and nephews were visiting for the season and so they were already helping out. Sometimes it was because business was slow. Sometimes it was because they had just hired one of the Patel boys from down the road and if only I had come in sooner, they would have done a proper interview. Sometimes it was because Ione and I were awfully young and they didn't want to get in trouble with the authorities for violating any labor laws.

But the last part was the same in every shop.

"I am so sorry, Cordelia."

* * *

Then we went to old Mr. Doyle's shop.

Seven Tears to the Sea was painted only a dull shade of brown. No awnings or carvings to make it look pretty. The sign out front proclaimed:

SELKIE SIGHTINGS
"Dangerous beasties of the sea"
GUARANTEED

The storefront also contained a small gift shop so Mr. Doyle could find yet another way of separating folks from their cash.

"I don't like him, Cordie. I don't like Mr. Doyle. I think I hate him," Ione said as we stood outside of his store. He'd not yet flipped the handwritten CLOSED sign around and opened up for the day, which was unusual considering it was getting close to eleven o'clock.

"You do not hate him. He's just old and cranky."

"He's mean, too. Mum didn't like him, either."

That was the thing about Mum. Most folks in the town loved her. She had that kind of personality that drew people to her like bees to honey. Most people, anyway. Mr. Doyle glared at her just like he glared at everyone else. He didn't find her that special at all. He just liked things the way he liked them and he didn't appreciate anyone telling him anything different. That's what Da said about him.

The door swung open and there was Mr. Archibald Doyle. If ever there was a person whose face looked like a puffer fish, it was Mr. Doyle.

"What are you kids doing on my porch?" His voice was gravelly, just what you'd expect from a talking puffer fish.

"Hi, Mr. Doyle. It's me, Cordelia Sullivan."

"I know who you are."

My own throat hurt at the roughness of his voice.

"Oh w-w-well . . ." I stuttered.

I swallowed and tried to remember my little speech, the one I'd said four times over, about wanting to work or do odd jobs for whatever pay he could spare, when Neevy picked this exact moment to begin what looked to be an epic fit.

"Hurry up and be about your business. Got a shop to keep here and I can't waste my day listening to a baby squall like it's being stuck with a pin." He moved his arms, as if to shoo us away.

"It's hard to run your shop if people think it's still closed," I said, sliding past him into the store and deftly flipping the sign over to the OPEN side. I came back through the doorway with the biggest, most friendly smile plastered on my face that I could manage. "See? It just must have slipped your mind when you opened up this morning." Then I gave Ione a hard look. She rolled her eyes, but she got my meaning. She quickly picked up the crying Neevy and began to bounce her around.

Neevy loved to bounce. And with Ione distracted, I pressed ahead.

"Look, Mr. Doyle. I am hoping to make some money. Since our mother went away—"

"'Twas only a matter of time," he interrupted.

"Since Mum went away," I continued, "we need help with the bills. Please, sir, please could you find a job for us here at your shop? We'll work for whatever you can spare, doing whatever needs doing. Please, sir. We just want to help our da."

Mr. Doyle was quiet for a minute, stroking his prickly beard. How it didn't end up piercing his hand, I had no idea.

"Never thought I'd be helping out the Sullivan clan." He scrunched his eyebrows down and looked at me through squinted eyes. "The babe's not welcome. Too loud. Scare away the customers. People say they like babes, but it's a lie. They like clean-smelling, silent babes. And those don't exist."

He stood there, all quiet. I didn't know if he was done with us, or if he was about to give us another lecture. Instead, he just turned his back on us, saying over his shoulder, "Be on time tomorrow, Cordelia Sullivan. Or Ione Sullivan. Whichever of you it is that comes. Be on time."

The door slammed behind him.

"Do you suppose we should ask him what time he means?" Ione asked, taking a biscuit from her pocket and trying to give it to Neevy, who moved her head away like she was a spy and the biscuit was some kind of poison. She wasn't hungry, then. Probably wet.

"No. I'll just get here tomorrow when the other shops open. I'm sure that will be early enough."

I wanted to skip down the street. I had gotten a job! I would be able to help!

But I didn't skip.

It was like suddenly there was a little angry box inside of me. For the past two months, I'd had mostly only one feeling, and that was sad. But now, since I'd found the letter, there was this box inside of my head and I knew I didn't want to open it. Still, the lid creaked up a teeny bit. *Your children have to work instead of play. The children you left behind, Mum,* came hissing out. I shook my head so it would fly away, out of my ears.

But I could still hear it.

All the way back to our house, I could hear it.

The Scientist

DA WASN'T SMILING when he came home that night.

Neevy heard the door open and recognized the sound of his heavy footsteps and turned herself around on the carpet, her legs kicking rhythmically.

"Hello, little carpet swimmer," he said softly, reaching down to pet her head as if she were a dog. Neevy liked it and kicked her feet harder.

He walked past me and planted a quick kiss on the top of my head.

"Cordie," he said, "what's the news of the day?"

"Same as usual," I said.

"Cordie got a letter from the landlord. Oops, that was yesterday," Ione said.

I threw her a look. Why did she choose to remember that just now?

"I'll look at it later," Da said. I sighed with relief.

"Cordie has sold us into slave labor," Ione said. She was

stuffing a piece of banana into her mouth. I got a good view of mashed-up goo as she spoke.

Da looked at me to translate. He was used to Ione's habit of stretching the truth into fantastic tales. But I wasn't so sure she was wrong.

"We got jobs today. At Mr. Doyle's shop."

Still holding his toolbox, Da opened the fridge and looked at the near-empty shelves. He grabbed a wrinkled apple, then shut the door. Then he looked through the kitchen doorway, to the blue-painted table where the telephone sat, and then back at me. "You don't have to do it, you know."

Ione was sitting on the floor now, playing with Neevy. I knew she didn't want to do it, and that I didn't, either. Back when Mum was here, her tips from the ladies at the Mermaid's Tresses were always enough to help us get by. Selkie Bay isn't a rich town, but during tourist season, ladies would pay well for Mum's magical fingers. But there were no magical fingers bringing home tips anymore.

"Yeah. I think we'll do it. It's better than sitting around being bored all day," I said, trying to convince him that his daughters would actually have fun cleaning Mr. Doyle's dusty store.

Da exhaled loudly. "I just wish repairing boats paid more." He sat in his chair, balanced his apple under his chin, put his toolbox beside him, and began unlacing his work boots. Soon he'd be at the sink, scrubbing off the day's boat grime.

"Why don't you go back to being a scientist? Didn't you make lots of money then?" Ione asked.

Ione had no manners.

"*Ione!*" I warned. "Don't."

"It's true," Ione insisted.

"You don't even really know what you are talking about. It was before you were born. The research boat Da was on—"

"Is no longer funded." Da's voice was quiet as he slid his feet from the boots and then munched on his snack. His socks had holes. "It's in a shipyard somewhere, rusted and broken. Besides, the research we were doing on pixie seals was, well . . ."

"Was what?" I asked.

"The research was off base. We weren't able to find the pixie seal habitats we were looking for. The population was diminishing. There used to be lots of them out there, lots. That's probably where all those legends about Selkie Bay come from. It would have ended eventually anyway, even if I hadn't quit."

"You quit because you fell off the boat into the sea and almost drowned," Ione said. She was at it again, trying to get Da to tell the story of how he met Mum. It was her favorite story, but one I knew Da wouldn't tell us. Not anymore.

Except Da's voice began low, as it always did when he told the story. I felt a tingling in my stomach and I held my breath. I felt for the letter in my pocket, as if touching it could somehow make him speak the words that would connect us to Mum once again. And then he started: "I was a scientist, not a sailor. Never quite steady with a boat beneath my feet. Spent a lot of my time half-leaned over the edge, puking. So there I was, pulling my head back up from a nice lean-over when something came out from between two nearby jagged rocks and bumped us, and over the edge I fell."

Ione's eyes were shining. She had gotten her way. Da was, for a moment, like he'd been before Mum left. I wanted to go and sit next to Ione, right at Da's feet, but I was afraid to move, afraid I would ruin whatever magic was causing Da to be his old self again.

"And with all of my expensive recording equipment strapped to me, I sank like a stone."

Even little Neevy crawled over to Da's chair. She had the decency not to start squalling.

"But then . . ." Ione said, leading Da to the best part. Da sighed and swallowed and I thought he might stop.

"But then, as I passed all kinds of rocks and seaweed, nearly making it to the very bottom of the seafloor, where I was sure I would die, I felt something around me. Smooth arms that somehow saved me."

"Mum!" Ione cried. I was afraid it might break the spell, saying her name, but Da continued.

"Yes, your mum. She was a fine, fair swimmer and she saved me. It was a coincidence she was close by. But coincidences happen in life, don't they? That's why there's a word for them."

He was silent then. There was more to the story, of course—how they fell in love, how they decided to settle in Selkie Bay because that's what Mum wanted.

But then Neevy burped, loud and juicy, and the enchantment was broken. The story that only moments earlier had floated in a mist around us now disappeared, seeping into the floorboards beneath us.

Nightmare

IONE WAS CRYING IN HER SLEEP, again.

I switched on my reading lamp, a small fixture with a turquoise shade that turned the room a soft, magical blue. The dim light reflected off her checks, pale and luminous, and a trail of silver tears glittered to her chin.

With her long dark hair and her thick lashes, she looked like Mum must have looked when she was eight. I crept out of my bed and walked the four steps it took to cross the room and clasped her hand in mine—long fingers with a thin half-moon of webbing at the base of each one. She must have gotten her hands from Mum. My fingers were short and stubby, like Da's.

"It's all right, Ione," I whispered, snuggling under the lavender bedspread. Ione loved purples; almost everything on her side of the room was some shade of purple. I wasn't so particular about colors myself, but I did love the aqua pillowcases Mum let me pick out for my birthday last year.

They made me feel like I was sleeping in a mermaid's bed. Gently, I maneuvered myself so that I could have a corner of Ione's pillow. She didn't give up much space, but it would have to do. I left the lamp on to comfort us both. When the light was on, I could almost convince myself that things would be all right again somehow. Night was always worse than the days.

Ione sobbed softly, so I started humming an old song that Da used to sing.

> *Away, away,*
> *We'll float away*
> *On a ship of gold.*
> *We'll sail.*

> *The silvery waves*
> *The salty spray*
> *The sea is calling*
> *Let's go today.*

I stopped humming when I got to that part, the part about going today. *Why had Mum left? What had called Mum away?*

I doubted it was the sea.

The hinges on that little angry box inside of me began to open.

"Don't stop, Cordie," Ione whispered. "Please. When you hum it always makes me sleepy."

"I don't feel much like it anymore," I said quietly. "Just go back to sleep. It's going to be okay." *Was it really better knowing that she hadn't wanted to go away?*

"Is she ever going to come back?"

I wanted to tell her yes, but I felt strange about it. *I will try to come back,* she'd written. *Try.* But why wasn't she here with us now? People have choices, don't they?

The angry lid opened a little more.

"It's going to be okay," I said again, hoarsely.

"But what if she never comes back?"

I swallowed. "Then I'll be here for you. Always."

"But I want *her.* I want Mum."

"Well, you can't have her!" I was too tired, too sharp, and I let that little box fly open, though I regretted it immediately. That's the thing about angry words—once you spill them out, they are like a broken jar of honey on the floor, all sticky and messy. And no matter how hard you try to clean it up, you can always feel that sticky part of the tile.

Naturally, Ione started crying again, even harder.

I pulled the old selkie book from the table between our beds.

"Shhh, I'm sorry. Ione, don't cry. Here, I'll read to you." I flipped to a page with a mother selkie surrounded by tiny baby seals and started to read.

Selkies make the most devoted of spouses and parents. Truly, no love on earth exists like that between a Selkie mum and her pups. Unless, of course, the Selkie has fallen in love with a human and the children are land-born. In this situation, the mother will stay dutifully with her children until she finds her sealskin coat. Then, despite the love she feels for her babes, she is compelled to return to the sea. There has been some reported success from the well-known trick of crying seven tears into the sea to entice a Selkie to return, though it is far from a dependable method—

"This is just boring," Ione interrupted, sobbing. "Boring doesn't make me feel better. It just makes me feel worse. Like Mum left because she didn't love us. Why doesn't she love us, Cordie?"

It was the most pitiful question you could imagine, asked in the most pitiful voice I'd ever heard Ione use.

Something happened inside of me, right there, right then. Something clicked, like the tiny light switch of the tiniest flashlight in the world. *I'd been truthful with Ione, mostly anyway, and it hadn't helped a bit.* For an instant I thought of showing her the note, but knowing Ione, she'd get her knickers in a twist because Mum hadn't left her a note, too. There had to be another way to give her some hope.

"She loves you, Ione. Mum loves all of us. But she can't come here because she's . . . in a special place," I said, testing the feel of the lie in my mouth. It didn't taste as bad as I expected.

"You mean she's . . . ?" Ione was on the verge of wailing now, threatening to wake the whole neighborhood.

"No, she's not dead. Remember the story of how Mum saved Da?"

Ione nodded and wiped her nose on the sheet before I could stop her.

"Well, you don't know the whole story, the true one. I might be the only one besides Mum who knows it."

"I want to know it, too," said Ione.

And so I told her the absolutely true story about Mum.

Except that I made the whole thing up, right there, on the spot.

How Mum Met Da

Mum was special, just ask anyone in the town. There was something about her. Of course, what they probably noticed was that she kept a secret. There's something about a person who is hiding the truth. You can't see a secret like that, or even smell it, but if you listen close enough, you can hear it. It whispers in the wind, from one person to the next.

Mum's eyes were the blackest of black, and her hair darker than night. And remember how, in between her fingers, there was lots of skin, almost like a frog's flippers? That's why she didn't like to shake hands with people—she didn't want them to see her hands. And then there was her coat, the one she hung in the closet, of the softest silver-black fur. If you did the math and added things up, well, you'd be suspicious. At least a little.

Mum wasn't from around here. She only moved to Selkie Bay a little before she met Da. She didn't tell anyone where she came from, but some guessed. They thought she came from the island, the one out there, the one she tried to show us that day in the boat.

That island is a mystery. Some people can't even see it, did you know that? But we can see it, because we have the same blood as Mum. That island hides a secret, too. It's where Mum's people are from.

But what I haven't said, not really anyway, is that Mum's people aren't really people. They aren't the same as everyone else. How do you think Mum managed to swim to the bottom of the sea and save Da? She could do it because she was a selkie. It's true, our mum can change shape from human to seal and back again, as long as she has her special coat.

You're probably waiting for the *once upon a time* part, so this will feel like a real story. Well, once upon a time, there was a selkie princess who was as beautiful as the moon is bright. She was sent to live among regular people because her father, the king of the selkies, told her she must.

"It is your duty as royalty to act as ambassador between the seal people and the land people. But you must keep it a secret. There are those who might not understand about a person who can change into a seal and back again in the blink of an eye," he said. That is why she never told anyone the truth about herself. Folks might not understand.

So she lived in Selkie Bay in a little house by herself, the same one we are living in now. She liked to collect small, fine things, like perfume bottles and silver saltshakers. Whatever she could find at the bottom of the sea and bring back home—for you know, selkies love to go shopping for treasure in shipwrecks.

But she was lonely. She missed her family. She knew that if it were really an emergency, she could call them by shedding seven silver tears into the sea, just like the book said. That's probably where Mr. Doyle got the idea for the name of his shop.

Anyway, there was Mum, the selkie princess, all lonely, out for an afternoon swim in the storm, for selkies don't fear storms at all. They are very brave. You can be brave like a selkie, too, Ione. That courage is just hiding inside of you, and if you stop crying long enough, it will find its way out.

Speaking of crying, well, there was our da, being washed over the side of his boat. He never liked the water much, but he loved seals. Isn't it a coincidence, then, that the man who loved seals gets saved by one? He cried seven tears because he was sick to his stomach from the waves and because he couldn't unstrap his equipment, not because he was a coward. Crying doesn't make someone a coward, don't ever think that. Crying just makes it hard to know what you are thinking. It clogs up your brain.

And if you are swept overboard by a wave, you need an unclogged brain to save yourself.

Luckily, Mum could smell the tears in the water. She didn't know whose they were, but that didn't matter. She knew she had to help. So she did.

And so she saved him. But she never told him her secret. She never told him what I told you, about the sealskin coat, and the kingdom of the selkies on that isle. Because that's probably where she is right now. Every few years, a selkie has to go back and be with her seal family for a while. That's the way it has to be. She has to report to her father, the king, about the land people. And I guess that takes a little time.

But she'll be back, Ione.

Of course she will.

Seven Tears to the Sea

I DECIDED THAT I WOULD BE THE FIRST to go and help out at Mr. Doyle's. I wasn't really the braver of the two of us, but I didn't want Ione starting a fight with the old grump. We needed the money, and I couldn't chance having her leave in a huff. What was Mum thinking, hiding that sugar jar of money away from all of us, anyway? Why didn't she just tell Da where she'd put it before she left? It was the least she could have done.

I yawned as I mixed a thin cereal for Neevy's breakfast. Ione could eat the other half of the banana she started yesterday. It was brown and speckled on the outside, but the inside was still okay. I wasn't even hungry yet—being too tired from not getting much sleep.

Da had left before it was light, which was very early considering it was summer and all. He'd knelt by my bed and whispered, "Good luck at Doyle's," which was his way of saying that although he wished it weren't necessary, it kind of was.

After feeding her the usual unappetizing bowl of mush, I dumped Neevy, desperately in need of a diaper change, on top of a sleeping Ione. A *Child's Book of Selkies* peeked out from under her flowery pillowcase.

"Oof," Ione groaned.

"That's what you get for sleeping so long. I'm going to Mr. Doyle's. I'll be back at lunch," I said. "See you later."

I could hear Ione and Neevy starting a game of peek-a-boo as I left. Hopefully, Ione would change the diaper before it leaked and she'd have to wash all her sheets. Oh well.

I was dreading my morning. It was a windy day, but even so the twenty-minute walk to town passed in seconds. The shop looked dark on the inside and the CLOSED sign hadn't been flipped. Maybe Mr. Doyle wasn't there yet. All I could see as I tried to peek through the dingy window were some small ceramic seal figurines that lined the window ledge. Would he make me dust them all? The thought of going home right at that moment felt very good. But then I wouldn't be able to bring home the money, so I reached for the knob of Seven Tears to the Sea and gave it a turn.

As I pushed the door open, a bell sounded in the store.

"In a minute!" called a gruff voice. Mr. Doyle, no doubt.

The inside of the shop was just as brown and boring as the outside. There were mermaid piggy banks lined up on one table and small stuffed seals with evil-looking faces on another. All in all, the store was no bigger than our sitting room, and not much different from it, except that there was a cash register along one wall and a sign that hung over the hallway that said TO THE BOATS with an arrow pointing to some steps on the right.

"Interested in a tour, are you?"

I jumped a little, and then turned quickly, face-to-face with Mr. Doyle.

"*You?*" he asked. "What are you doing here?"

Had he forgotten about hiring me? My face felt hot, even though it was no fault of mine if he had made a mistake.

"Um . . . yesterday, you said I should come and help at the shop."

"I said what?"

I knew he had heard me, from the way his own face reddened. But I could tell he wanted me to repeat it, so I did.

"You hired me to help in the shop."

He was quiet as he looked me up and down. He didn't like me one bit.

"Did I now?"

"Yes. You did," I replied. I stood straighter, just as straight as Mum had when she'd stood up to him months ago, when she took us out in the boat and he stood on the beach, shaking his head at us all.

Mr. Doyle glared for a moment, then rubbed his chin.

"Fine. Start over there." He pointed to tall wooden

shelves, stuffed full of old books and random objects, and handed me a ratty cloth. "Dust."

For the next three hours, I dusted Mr. Doyle's shelves, which apparently hadn't been cleaned for a hundred years, while he rummaged around looking for stuff he couldn't find. I had to ask for a new rag twice, for they got filthy quickly, and dusting with a blackened cloth just moves the dirt around instead of picking it up. We didn't talk, or whistle, or hum. The only noise was the sound of his feet as he shuffled about the place, and my occasional sneeze.

"Done?" Mr. Doyle asked as I came down from the chair I'd been standing on so I could get to the layers of grime on the top of the bookcase. I started to smile a bit proudly, for it was a big job that I'd just finished, when he pointed to the table with the mermaid piggy banks. "Now you can start on that one. Straighten it up, and try to make room for more without making it look like a junk pile. Lots of folks will be interested in these." He picked up one of the evil-looking seals. "Had these selkies made overseas for almost nothing. They'll be hot sellers when the tourists come."

"That doesn't look much like a selkie," I said before I could stop myself.

"*What?*"

I wanted to bite my tongue, or kick myself in the pants. Mr. Doyle looked like he wanted to kick me in the pants, too. "I mean, it just kind of looks like an angry seal," I mumbled, remembering the beautiful pictures in *A Child's Book of Selkies*.

"As if you know what a selkie looks like!" he muttered. Then the wrinkles around his eyes crinkled up and he laughed. It wasn't a jolly-sounding laugh, but a cross between a cough and a wheeze. "You wouldn't recognize a selkie if it was right under your nose, Cordelia Sullivan! Now, get to work," he ordered.

So I did.

I tried to make a pyramid from some of the little stuffed gray creatures. They were awful-looking, like they had fangs or something.

"That'll do," said Mr. Doyle. "That'll give me room for these!" And he plopped down a massive stack of booklets with titles like *How to Spot a Selkie* and *The History of the Selkie Beasties*.

I thought of Mum then. She was just so beautiful. And I remembered her telling such tales to me, about the selkies, tales from the old book. *She* was the only one who could make those old stories come alive for me. Without her voice reading the lore of the selkies, the whole thing just sounded ridiculous—to think that people could change into seals and back again.

And I felt stupid for filling Ione's head with it all.

But Ione was old enough to know better, old enough to figure out I was just making it all up.

"Reading something interesting, Cordelia Sullivan?" Mr. Doyle barked, startling me into dropping a booklet. I hastily picked it up and put it in the stack.

"No." I stacked the booklets neatly into four piles.

"You'd do well to stay away from them, selkies I mean. Oh, I know, folks say they're just a legend. But if folks truly believed that, there'd be no horde of tourists in Selkie Bay at the close of each summer, now, would there? Folks say they don't exist," he said, his voice for once softer and smoother than butter melting on sliced bread. "But we know different, don't we?"

Mr. Doyle winked a wrinkly wink.

I stood there, still as stone.

"Whatcha waiting for, girl? You don't expect me to pay you after just one day, do you?"

"Um—er—" I stammered. I wanted to ask him what he meant, and why he'd winked like we shared some kind of joke, which I was sure we didn't, when he thrust some bills into my hand and then almost shoved me out of the store. "All right then. Have your money. Your work for the day is finished."

Fever

WHEN I GOT HOME, Da was there already. Da never came home early.

Neevy was sick.

"Why didn't you call me?" I asked Ione as I marched into the house, past Da, who was holding Neevy close to his heart.

I could see her chest rise and fall. But she wasn't moving much.

"I wasn't going to call old Mr. Doyle. And I was afraid to walk to town and leave Neevy. And I couldn't very well carry her with me in this wind, could I?" Ione sassed back. "I called Da at the docks. After five times someone finally answered. And he came."

Da was cooing to Neevy, and she was listening, I think.

Ione was already cooking the broth on the stove. The same kind Mum always made when this happened. At least she'd thought enough to do that.

"Neevy, little one, wake up," Da whispered in Neevy's ear, though I could hear it across the room. I walked over and touched her head, praying with all my soul she wasn't hot.

She was.

"Da," I said, "I think she's got the fever again."

I hadn't wanted to say it. Neevy's fevers were strange. They used to worry us sick when she was first born. Neevy would turn red as a beet and her dark eyes would be large and glassy. She wouldn't cry or eat—she'd just lie there limply.

"Maybe we should take her to the doctor," I said even though I knew there would be no money to pay the medical bill. And besides, the doctors never did much for her. They always said the fever would just run its course. Unless it didn't. Then we were to bring her in again.

"In the morning," he said. "If the fever hasn't broken, we'll take her in the morning."

I nodded across the room to Ione, who poured the broth into a small bowl.

It was going to be a long night.

* * *

The fever was still raging when Ione and I turned in. I hadn't wanted to go to bed, but Ione wouldn't go without me. I knew that she needed her sleep if she was to go and help Mr. Doyle the next day, and I knew that we needed money, especially if we had to pay the doctor now, so going to bed seemed like the smartest thing to do.

Of course, Ione wanted another selkie tale about Mum. With Neevy being sick, I didn't have it in me to argue. So I told her how our selkie mum took care of her little cousin selkie pups during a horrible storm, how she stayed with them on the island so the other selkies could go save shipwrecked sailors, and how the sailors repaid the selkies in treasure. At some point during the telling, I was so tired I wasn't sure what I was saying anymore. But by that time, Ione was fast asleep.

At about midnight, I crawled out of my bed, crept into the sitting room, and there Da sat by the hearth, still holding Neevy in his arms.

Mum's rocking chair creaked a little as I slid into it.

"Da," I said, rocking back and forth only the tiniest bit, like Mum used to. "What are you thinking?"

He was quiet. I thought he hadn't heard me, but before I could ask again, he said, "I am just thinking about . . . things."

"Do you think she'll be okay?" I asked.

"Neevy? Yes, I think she'll be okay. She's feeling cooler. But I think she needs . . ." His voice trailed off.

"Mum," I finished for him. "Neevy needs Mum."

There were no words he could say, so he just nodded.

He held my baby sister there for a moment, gently rubbing her forehead.

"And how was your day, Cordelia?" he asked.

He was a master at changing the subject.

"Oh, fine." I got up, walked to the small bookshelf where I'd stashed my meager pay from earlier. "Here's this," I said, handing him Mr. Doyle's wrinkled bills.

He took them without even counting them and nodded, like he was trying to say *thanks* but couldn't get the word to come out.

As I sat down again I must have scooted the chair over, for the floorboards underneath Mum's rocker groaned. It was as if the chair or the floor or maybe even the house itself was daring me to fill the empty space between Da and me with words. Not just any words—questions. For a few seconds, I felt brave.

"Are you mad at her?" I asked Da for the very first time since she'd left.

"Neevy?" he replied, even though he knew I hadn't meant Neevy.

"No," I said, my own tiredness adding to my courage. "I meant Mum. Are you mad at her for leaving?"

Da was quiet. Then he shook his head from side to side.

"No, Cordelia," he whispered, "how could I be mad at her?"

"What if she needed your help or something? Would you go help her?"

"Your mother doesn't need anyone's help, Cordie." His voice cracked and I knew I had pushed too far.

"I'm sorry, Da, I—"

"Your mum is strong, the strongest person I ever knew. She always was. If there was something she thought needed to be done, then she just did it, no question. Your mum is strong," he repeated. "Like you, Cordie."

Daughter of the Selkie

IN THE MORNING, I assured Da I could look after Neevy on my own and sent him to work. She had no fever when she woke. So I bundled her in a couple of soft, faded blankets and laid her gently in the pram. She was a sleepy thing this morning.

"Hurry up, Ione," I said, stuffing some bread in the toaster. I didn't feel great about Ione walking all the way to town by herself, so I'd offered to accompany her. True, during the school year she often walked home alone, since we got out at different times. But that was before.

She munched her toast loudly instead of talking to me as we walked to town. And when we got there, she went grudgingly off to help Mr. Doyle. I'd made sure she looked presentable, which included dressing her in her cleanest shirt (the purple one with stripes) and attempting to brush her tangled hair. I had warned her numerous times not to be a pain. And all during the walk, she didn't mention the selkie stories I told her about Mum, so I didn't, either.

"Be good, Ione," I called as she turned the knob to his store. She whipped her head around and stuck her tongue out at me. There were toast crumbs all around her mouth, but it was too late to do anything about it.

I was left with a sleeping lump of a baby in the pram. I wheeled her across the street to the Mermaid's Tresses, but there was Maura's sign, CLOSED UNTIL THE 1ST, taped to the front of the door. So I found my way to a tourist throne— that's what we called the benches that lined the harbor and faced the water—and sat for a bit.

It was early, but not too early for the shops to open. Flip-per's Fast-Mart was always first. You could smell their coffee all the way down the street. Most of the shopkeepers went in for a cup, even those who liked tea better. The town moved slowly today, not like it would in a few weeks when August hit. Then the light traffic of those out for a morning stroll would be replaced by the bustle of families, all hoping for a summer swim, a harbor tour, or maybe a glimpse of a selkie.

Even though the brisk air of the morning felt good to me, Neevy gave a little shiver. Her cheeks were deep pink, not the healthy pink of a laughing baby, but the reddish pink of a baby who's not feeling well.

And her lips were pale. I felt her head.

Fever.

I started quickly toward home. I thought about going to find Da at the other side of the harbor, at the workmen's dock, where the tourists never went because rusted-out boats in dry-dock didn't look all that pretty. But it was a long walk past a couple of pubs that weren't as fancy as the three named after the pirate queen. Maura said they were seedy and to steer clear. I hadn't liked it one bit when I'd had to walk there before. Besides, I didn't want Da to have to leave work early again.

So I hurried home. As I jogged, Neevy bounced gently in the pram, but didn't stir.

* * *

Neevy's fever continued throughout the morning, and into the afternoon. I kept trying to feed her water and milk, but she liked neither.

At two o'clock, Ione burst through the door. "Oh, Cordie, you'll never guess what I did!"

"Well, you're a couple of hours late. Where have you been?" I asked, keeping Neevy covered up so Ione wouldn't see her red arms and worry about the fever. Ione was too much of a worrier as it was.

"That Mr. Doyle is . . . well . . . weird," Ione said. She went to the kitchen and took a piece of bread and ate it hungrily. I had forgotten to put it away after I tried to feed it to Neevy. It was probably a little stale, but at least someone would eat it and I hadn't wasted it. I needed to remember to take better care of things.

"What work did he make you do?" I asked. "I had to dust, stack stuffed animals, and arrange pamphlets yesterday."

"Well, at first he just squinched his eyes up tight and looked at me, like I was a frog or something. He said that if he didn't know better, he would think he was looking right at a young selkie, what with my eyes and hair being so dark and all. And then I told him 'Well, that's because my mum is a selkie, but it's a secret. So don't tell.'"

"You told him *what?*" I stood up, nearly dropping Neevy. She roused, fussed a little, then went back to sleep.

"I know it was a secret, but, Cordie, you won't believe what he said."

"Let's hear it," I said, knowing what was coming next. He must have told Ione what an idiot she had for a big sister. He must have told her that her sister had told her a big fat lie. Both of which points, at this moment, were true.

"He said '*I knew it!*' and he slapped his leg, like I'd just told him a joke. '*I knew it! I knew it!*' He danced around. I didn't know he could move like that. He looked really funny. So I laughed. And, Cordie, Mr. Doyle laughed, too!"

Mr. Doyle was not capable of laughter. There was some kind of mistake.

"He wanted the details then, so I told him all I could remember. And I told him about the old book and he asked if he could borrow it, so of course I said yes. You know, I think I was wrong about him. I don't hate him, after all. And then, oh, we had so much fun."

I was getting a little mad at Mr. Doyle. Sure, he hadn't called me a liar and told Ione that there were no such things as selkies. He hadn't crushed the tiny hope that I had given her.

But maybe it would have been better if he had.

"He took me out on his boat, Cordie. The one he gives tours on. He says he's going to make a big sign for me to hold and put me right out in front of his store. Then we chugged all around the harbor in his tour boat, even though it smells like car smoke. He said it would be good for business to have a selkie girl seen riding in his boat. Cordie! Don't you see? Mr. Doyle thinks I might actually be a selkie, too!"

And this was the moment I knew it had gone too far.

"Ione, calm down." My voice was gentle and quiet, so quiet, in fact, that it actually got Ione's attention.

"What's the matter, Cordie? Why are you like this?" she whined. Then her eyes got wide. "Did you hear something from Mum?"

I felt my pocket for the letter to make sure it was still hidden, and took a deep breath.

"Ione, the stories I told you, well, they were just stories. You know that, right? You are not a selkie. Mum is not—"

Ione flipped her hand at me, brushing me off. "I knew you'd say that. Mr. Doyle told me you might."

"Ione—"

She wasn't listening. She was at the sink filling a glass with water, turning the tap all the way on to drown me out.

"I mean you were right," she went on. "Of course she's a

selkie. Otherwise, why did she leave?" Ione whipped around and faced me again and within one second, she had gone from bubbly to heartbroken. "Because she doesn't love us? She does love us, doesn't she?" she asked, the tears coming.

"Of course she does."

"Then we have to try and get her to come back," Ione wailed.

* * *

And that's how we ended up back at the shorefront that afternoon, feverish baby and all, the midsummer wind whipping at our cheeks and tugging at the ends of our hair, except for Neevy, of course. Facing west toward the waves, we stood and did the only thing we could think to do to get our mum to return. The only thing the legends said would summon a selkie. It was Ione's idea, and I just didn't have it in me to say no. It would have looked strange to passersby, so luckily there weren't any. Just us, the three Sullivan girls, crying our seven silver tears into the sea and letting them float atop the foam, hoping they would bring our mum back to us.

Alone

WHEN DA GOT HOME we ate a simple meal of soup and cheese sandwiches. Mum hadn't liked cheese sandwiches, but the rest of us could never get enough of them.

"There's an old boat that needs restoring at a museum over in Glenbay," Da said finally, as if testing the words on his tongue. "The money is good, very good in fact, but I feel bad leaving you girls all alone." He paused and took a spoonful of soup. "It wouldn't be for long, a couple of days maybe." He didn't have to say that we needed the money. We all knew it. And it wasn't the first time his work had taken him away from Selkie Bay, just the first time since Mum left. "I could have Maura watch over you." He gestured toward town with his soup spoon. "I'll phone her about it tonight."

Ione started to protest, but I kicked her under the table, not hard, but just enough to get her attention. "I'll do it, Da. I'll talk to Maura tomorrow for you."

Da took a bite of his sandwich and looked over at Ione, whose eyes were watering from the kick. *Such a drama queen.*

I gave her a look. A hard, hard look. *Shut up or he'll find out Maura's gone and then he won't be able to go.*

"But, Cordie—" she blurted out, cheese and chewed bread completely visible. If I could have shot lightning bolts out of my eyes and fried Ione's tongue into silence, I would have.

"It'll be fine." I was smiling too much, in that forced way where your cheeks do all the work, pulling your mouth up and crinkling your eyes, like the happiness is real.

Da turned to me and said, "If you could do that, Cordie, if you could talk to Maura about looking after you girls, it will save me from having to find time to do it."

He turned back to his dinner and I glared at Ione, praying that she wouldn't ruin this. Then she started to smile, the real kind of smile. She probably thought our little trick at the dock would bring Mum waltzing back through the door. Thankfully, at least she was silent.

"Sure, Da. I'll see to it in the morning."

True, I didn't like lying, but I was a practical person—a person who does what needs to be done (like making up stories for Ione that she needs to hear, even though I worried about making a big mess of it all) and what needed to be done now was Da going off to Glenbay and making lots of money, and Ione and me looking after ourselves.

And Neevy, too.

". . . and Neevy looks better," Da was saying. I nodded, trying to pay attention. Neevy was on a blanket on the floor nearby, playing with a large rubber spoon from the kitchen. "How's the fever?"

"Gone, I think," I said. This time I was telling the truth. Neevy was better this evening than she had been this morning. But maybe it helped that the night was bringing a cool, salty breeze to the house from the nearby sea. Neevy always seemed more active when the air had a chill. And a thick, moist fog was rolling in.

"Good," Da said. "I'm catching a ride with Old Jim to Glenbay in the morning. Can't imagine him on those winding roads in a fog like this." Da rose, went to the sink, washed his bowl, then proceeded to sort through his toolbox, making sure he had the things he needed for the job.

"I'll clean up," I told Ione. "Why don't you play with Neevy for a bit?"

Ione hated chores, so she rose and swept Neevy away to the sitting room before I could change my mind. I gathered the bowls and plates from the table and began to wash them, debating with myself whether I had the courage to tell Da about the lies I'd told to Ione. The big, fat, selkie lies. It had been wrong and I knew it. I just didn't know how to get out of it. I didn't know how to tell her the truth and make her believe me, without making everything worse.

Except that if I told Da, then he'd know I was a person who told lies, and he might figure out that I was lying about having Maura watch over us. I was staring out the window over the sink, trying to organize my jumbled brain when Da said, "Cordie, you all right? The water's been running an awful long time."

I quickly shut off the tap and turned to face him. He was squatting on the floor of the small kitchen, right in front of the toolbox. That's when I saw it.

"What's that?" I asked, even though I knew exactly what it was. *Mum's sugar jar.* Sitting right there, in Da's box.

"Um, it's just an old jar. It holds . . . things . . . screws, nails . . ."

"It's not just a jar. That's the sugar jar. And I know what's inside of it."

My voice was shaking and my finger was out in front of me, pointing like crazy. It was shaking, too.

"Cordie, what are you talking about?" His voice was quiet, like he didn't want Ione to hear, because he probably didn't.

"That jar is full of money. I know because Mum's note told me."

"You have a note from your mother?"

I nodded and pulled it from my pocket. It was wrinkled and soft and my trembling hand held it like an old branch holds a dry leaf.

He was trembling, too. But he read it, folded it, then handed it back.

"How could you, Da? How could you let us work for Mr. Doyle if you had the money?"

"Cordie, I . . ."

But he didn't say anything else. He just sat there on the floor of the kitchen, looking down at the jar in the toolbox. Then he reached in, picked it up, and handed it to me.

It was heavy.

I opened it. It was filled with money. Lots of money. The bottom was heavy with coins, but the top overflowed with all kinds of paper money.

"Why, Da? Why don't you use it to pay the bills? Wouldn't Mum have wanted you to pay the bills?"

"Sometimes there are more important things than money," was all he said.

"What's that supposed to mean?"

He shrugged and I could tell he was climbing into that place inside of himself where he didn't talk to anyone. But I was too mad to let him retreat into his little chamber of silence.

"Why does every grownup in this house have to lie to me? Why does one disappear far away and the other disappears right here, right in front of my eyes?"

Da stood then and put his hands on my shoulders. "Hold

on to the money, Cordie, I hope you won't need it while I am gone, but just in case."

I wanted to let the jar drop to the floor and shatter into a million pieces.

But I held it.

"I was keeping it for a reason, Cordie. I can't tell you because I made a promise, although I am beginning to wonder if it was a very smart one to make. There are things I can't tell you, and even if I could, I am not sure how."

His hands were firm, like he was trying to send the secrets he could not speak down through his arms and into me.

But if he was too much a coward to say them, then I was too angry to try to understand them. Instead, I stuffed the jar under my shirt so Ione wouldn't see it and went into my room.

"Cordie . . ." I heard him say, but I didn't turn around.

The Empty Hanger

WITH THE DAWN LIGHT just peeking through the window, I felt Da's kiss on my forehead and his whispered, "Goodbye, Cordie. See you in a couple days." I pretended to still be asleep as Old Jim and his rattley car arrived to pick up Da.

As the sound of the car faded, I got out of bed and began to search for a place to hide the sugar jar. I couldn't leave it where Ione might stumble upon it, and there were no hiding places in our room that she didn't know about. The coat closet in the hall, however, didn't get much use, with it being summer and all. The door barely creaked when I opened it. The barren high shelf seemed too obvious, so I knelt down, searching for . . . what? I wasn't sure.

"That's where it used to hang, isn't it? Her coat. The one that changed her back into a seal," Ione said, sneaking up on me as I sat on the floor moving Neevy's foldable pram and some old boxes. She flicked the empty hanger with her fingers and it made tiny squeaks while it swung back and forth.

Well, now I couldn't hide anything in there. "Why are you up already? And why do you always follow me?" I snapped.

"Why do you have to be so mean?" Ione said, sinking to the floor beside me. She gave a big sigh. It was going to be a moody day.

I was mad, but still I reached out and patted her hair like Mum would have done. "Don't start. Let's not fight today."

She sniffled and wiped her nose on the sleeve of her pajamas. "You are right. We shouldn't fight, not with Mum on her way back."

I wished that Neevy would wake up and start crying and that we'd forget we were ever sitting in this stupid closet. But Neevy was silent.

"What were you doing in here, Cordie?" Ione asked, as if it had finally occurred to her that it was strange to see me on my hands and knees rummaging around on the closet floor. "And why do you have the sugar jar?" Faster than I could stuff it behind me, Ione swiped it and jerked the lid off.

"Oh my gosh." Ione's eyes were as large as cereal bowls as she took the thick wad of bills from the jar. "Cordie, how did you—?"

Neevy started crying up a storm, too late to save me, of course. Ione couldn't stop looking at the money in her hand, so I grabbed it and rewadded up the bills. "Go and get her," I said.

"But, Cordie—" Ione whispered, even though there was no one in the house who could hear us but Neevy, who couldn't understand, anyway. "What—how—?"

"I'll tell you later," I said. "Now go and get her before she tries to climb over the rail of the crib again."

Ione nodded and got up. She must have been in shock, because she actually listened to me, then looked back twice before she turned the corner of the short hallway and made her way to Neevy's room.

How to explain . . .

Was this how Da felt last night when *I* discovered the money?

* * *

"She's all fresh now," said Ione, who had changed our sister impossibly fast and was now smiling like a cat who has just discovered a gallon of cream. "And hungry."

I popped two pieces of bread in the toaster for Ione and me. Neevy was quiet while I made her a bowl of oatmeal, occupied and excited by the blandness that was to come. But I could feel Ione's eyes on me, waiting for me to say something.

"I've got to go to Mr. Doyle's today," I said, even though I didn't want to.

"Why? It's not like we need the money." Ione put Neevy in her little chair and began feeding her, first the oatmeal, then a bit of leftover applesauce. Neevy's spoon skills were horrible when she was left on her own. "We could even eat in a restaurant! You've got that jar—"

"That's not my money to use. Not for ordinary stuff, anyway."

"Did you steal it, Cordie? Did you steal it from somewhere and hide it in the closet?" Ione's voice was more curious than upset, as if it wouldn't have bothered her one bit if I'd stolen the money.

"I don't steal. But the money isn't ours to spend. Not really." I had no idea how far behind we were on the rent and the rest of the bills. This might not even catch us up. Besides, I couldn't stop wondering about what Da might have been saving it for. I took the spoon and Neevy's almost-empty bowl and began washing them in the sink. "You need to eat your breakfast now, Ione. And I am going to Mr. Doyle's."

"Maybe I should go instead. He said he needed a selkie girl—"

"I remember what he said. And no, you're not going. It's my turn." And Mr. Doyle was going to get a big, fat piece of my mind. "I'll hurry back for lunch and check on the both of you. Everything is going to be fine," I said.

"Of course it will. Mum will be here soon, remember? We cried the seven tears and all." Ione plopped herself at her usual spot at our small kitchen table and eyed her toast and jam distastefully, but took a few nibbles. In that moment, she didn't even look eight. She looked so little. So little and young and *filled with hope*.

79

"Ione," I said. "Mum is not . . . um . . . it will probably take a while for seven tears to travel all the way from the dock to the isle," I said before I could change my mind.

Sometimes it was just easier to go with it.

"But she came so quickly before, when she saved Da."

"Well, she was close by, swimming around like a selkie does. She was probably already in her sealskin."

"She's in her sealskin now, don't you think? Her coat is gone, after all. I used to love that coat. It was so soft."

"Yes, sealskins are very soft. I am sure Mum is in hers right now, swimming someplace far away, probably. Otherwise, don't you think she'd be looking in on us? Watching out for us from the bay?"

Ione looked up at the ceiling as she considered the logic of my argument. "No. She's probably on an island, or even farther north. Maybe she is hungry for crab."

I could still taste in my mouth the flavor of the lies I'd told yesterday. They tasted worse today. Bitter and sour. But I told myself it was all going to be fine. One thing at a time. I could deal with Ione and her "selkie" Mum after I'd found a hiding place for the money. Because if I knew Ione, she'd spend all morning searching for that jarful of cash. If she couldn't find it, maybe she'd forget about the whole thing.

* * *

"Oh, it's you again," Mr. Doyle said, as he opened the door to his shop just as I came up the steps.

"It is me that's here today, Mr. Doyle, and we need to have a talk." I shifted my weight from my left foot to my right, then uncomfortably back again. I'd stuffed all the money in my shoes, except for the coins, which I'd put in my pockets. That's all there was room for in the old jeans I was wearing. Not a penny left at home for Ione to find.

"I don't pay you to talk, Cordelia. I pay you to work," he grumbled, folding his arms across his chest and rolling his eyes. "Come inside and let's hear it so we can get on with what needs doing."

I followed him in and took a deep breath. I wanted to be diplomatic. At least I thought I did. But the moment I opened my mouth again to speak, the angry box flew open.

"How could you lie to my sister like that?"

His snort rattled around in his nostrils before it finally huffed out. "You're one to talk."

He had me there.

I scrambled for more ammunition. "So you admit that you made up a lie about Ione being a selkie girl?"

"I did nothing of the sort. You need to get your story straight, Miss Sullivan, before you go accusing people of things you don't seem to know much about. It's time maybe you heard the truth about Selkie Bay."

Mr. Doyle's Tale

Liars come in all shapes and sizes, young lady.

Sometimes folks think they are telling a lie to make things better. But then they are telling two lies. One to another person and one to themselves.

Most people think that selkies are some kind of magical, beautiful, half-human, half-seal creature who is both mystical and misunderstood . . . like a unicorn or that imaginary horse with wings.

But selkies are not beautiful or magical and they're not imaginary, either. Well, perhaps the shape-shifting part is magical, but only a small bit.

First and foremost, selkies are liars and thieves. I know this because they stole from me. And you should know about this, too, because your mum was one of them.

I've met three real and true selkies in my lifetime—at least three that I know of. Could have been more, for I might not have been paying attention all the time. The first was when I was a boy. I was with my da on an island nearby, taking care of the seal problem. And this isle, well, it wasn't like any I'd seen before. There were caves made for hiding treasure, and the whole thing was covered with seals.

Oh, the seals! They were eating all the fish in the bay and beyond! My da was fisherfolk—so you can see the problem. The fishermen kept returning from their trips with empty boats. So we did what the fisherfolk did in those days. We took care of the problem. Even a bull seal is no match for a man with a club. Don't look at me like that. Do you think I liked it? Do you think I enjoyed what I had to do? It was the most awful thing I've ever done, attacking those gray seals. Gives me nightmares to this day and still makes me sick when I wake, all cold and shaking.

So there we were, with our clubs. I was crying about it and my da was yelling at me to be a man. And then *she* came—a huge black seal, unlike any of the others. There was something about her eyes, fiery and unholy they were. Terrifying eyes. And I knew when I looked in them that she was not an ordinary seal. She was far too intelligent, the mind of a human in the skin of a seal. She chased us away. My da took one look at the demon seal, crossed himself, then turned to run. But he tripped over his own club and broke his leg. He was lying there in horrible pain and then the selkie was coming over to us.

I covered my face with my hands. I begged her not to hurt us. I could feel her hot breath against my cheek and I thought I was dead for certain.

But she left me unharmed. And when I opened my eyes, she was gone, and so were the rest of the seals. Gone with her, except for the hundreds of carcasses on the beach.

The seals have been gone ever since. Some scientists came out many years later, you may know about this, Cordelia, since your da was one of them. They wanted to find the seals that had vanished, the pixie seals they were called, to study them, but that project didn't pan out, as well you know.

The next selkie I met was in the form of a woman named Pegeen. Fell under her spell, I did, and married her. But soon she stole all my money and took off with it to that secret isle. I'm sure of it. Oh, I searched for her, and that island. I searched.

But this story is not about Pegeen, is it?

The third selkie I've met was your mum.

I didn't have to look twice at her to know that Rose Sullivan was one of the seal folk, being knowledgeable about them as I now was. We argued, your mum and I, about that island. I knew she lied about not knowing where it was. And we argued about my tour business. She said I was an exploiter. She said I took advantage of folks and lied to them. Lied! As if she was one to talk.

And now she's gone, Cordelia, because that's what selkies do. They leave. The sea calls them and they go.
Sure as the moon chases the sun from the sky each night,
I knew that mother of yours would leave. You'd better
watch that sister of yours, in case the sea calls her, too.
Calls her out to that island where the selkies hide their
treasures.

The Seal

"I DON'T BELIEVE IT. Any of it," I said.

"I didn't expect you would. Too much like your da," said Mr. Doyle.

"What does that mean?"

"It means them that's born with the blood of Selkie Bay in their veins know things that the rest of the world can't believe."

"I was born in Selkie Bay," I retorted.

"But you're not one of them. Ione, she might be. Remains to be seen."

I was beginning to think that Cranky Old Mr. Doyle was actually Crazy Old Mr. Doyle. "I don't want you taking Ione out on that boat of yours anymore."

"Legends all come from somewhere. In every fairy story you've ever heard there is a grain of truth. In this case, there is a jarful of it. A whole jar of truth."

I thought uncomfortably of the money jar and felt my cheeks start to burn.

"Don't think folks in the town haven't wondered about Ione, being your mum's daughter and all. People talk. I listen. I give the people what they want. I'm just trying to drum up more business. And more business means I can pay more to my employees. We are in this together, Cordelia."

The money in my shoes felt enormous, boosting me up, making me taller.

"Then I quit. And Ione does, too. We want no part of being ex- . . . exploiters," I said, using the grown-up word proudly. "What do you even show tourists dumb enough to go on that boat of yours? There are no more pixie seals and there are no selkies—"

"There's seals if you know where to look, out far enough, different kinds than the pixie. But they are out there. Besides, only a trained eye can tell the difference between a seal and a selkie, anyway. And for your information, it's not just the out-of-towners who are curious. There's folks in the town who'd swear on their mother's grave they've seen a selkie. They come to me for validation. For a small fee, I am happy to oblige."

I turned around then, and walked toward the door without looking back. But Mr. Doyle grabbed me by the arm.

"You know where it is, don't you? She told you. She told you where the island is. Where the treasure is."

"What treasure? I don't know what you are talking about. Leave me alone."

I flew out of his store and down the steps, only to bump into Ione, pushing the pram right in front of Mr. Doyle's shop.

"Cordie! Cordie! Cordie! You'll never guess!" she sang out, stopping the pram short, causing Neevy to jerk forward and drop the peeled banana she'd been feeding herself. By the look on her face, it didn't seem like much of the banana had actually gotten into her hungry little mouth.

"What are you doing here? I am guessing Neevy is better?" I asked, even though I knew there had to have been something else that drove her to push Neevy all the way into town.

Ione quickly grabbed the banana from the ground, pretended to dust it off, and then handed it back to Neevy.

"*Ione,*" I warned.

She shrugged, then felt Neevy's forehead with the back of her hand. "Nope. No fever. Not too hot at all," she said, even though she had no idea what *too hot* felt like.

I placed my own hand on Neevy's head for confirmation. True, she didn't feel warm. And she looked livelier than she had last night. I took control of the pram with one hand and Ione with the other, and walked us briskly away from Doyle's store.

"Has she been coughing?" I asked.

"Nope."

"All right then. I'll bite. What's got you so excited?"

We finally passed Chippy's, so it seemed okay to slow down a little. It always smelled best mid-morning, when they fried the first fish of the day. My stomach rumbled and I had to remind it that despite the bills in my shoes, I had no money to spend—none that was mine, anyway.

Ione had been waiting for me to ask her about the *you'll never guess*, but now that I finally had, she was silent for a moment or two. She looked hungrily at a couple of locals leaving Chippy's, clutching delicious golden morsels wrapped in newspaper—the traditional way to serve fish and chips.

"Why did you leave Mr. Doyle's?" she asked, having noticed at last that I'd left early.

"Tell you later," I said, hurrying her a little farther down the strip, farther away from the front of Mr. Doyle's miserable shop, and from the torturously delicious smell of Chippy's. We ended up in front of Whale of a Tale, where I sat on my favorite bench, one shaped like a dolphin. There was room for two, so I motioned for Ione to sit. "Now tell me why you are here."

"I'm afraid you're going to get mad."

"Did you let her flush something important?" I asked, though I was pretty sure that since Neevy was only now beginning to pull herself up, she hadn't figured out the handle on the toilet. Yet.

"No. It's just that I had to *see*, Cordie."

I sighed like Da does when there's something he doesn't want to deal with. "You know you weren't supposed to leave. What did you just have to see?"

Ione jumped up from the dolphin bench and spun around, her eyes bright and excited. She almost knocked into a long-haired man walking into the bookshop, but luckily he saw her first, doing a strange sort of side step to avoid her. I'd have laughed at their ridiculous dance, except there was something about the way Ione was carrying on that worried me, all the way to the center of my bones. "We went to the dock, over there. I wheeled Neevy down the bumpy old pier and I saw her, Cordie. I saw Mum."

My heart thudded. *She'd seen Mum?* I felt dizzy and hot and filled with all kinds of things, all of them bursting to get out, until I realized that, of course, she was mistaken. If she'd seen Mum, then Mum would be here right now, talking with us.

And she wasn't.

"And I figured out why she hasn't come back," Ione continued, having finished her festival of bouncing about, and now sitting close to me again, her voice a whisper. "It all makes sense now, Cordie. Perfect sense. She's stuck in her seal form."

Her seal form?

I had been so, so stupid filling her head with those selkie tales.

"See, there was a black seal, black and silvery gray just like mum's coat," Ione continued. "I knew it was her. She looked at me, Cordie. Right at me. When was the last time you saw a seal come into the bay like that? I'll tell you when. Never. Da always said that the people and their boats keep the seals away. But there she was! Right next to the dock. She's watching over us, Cordie."

I had no words for the feelings that swirled inside me. The angry box flew open and little mad meanies swarmed around in my head. This time, I was not only mad at Mum and Da, but at myself, too. *How could I have let this go on?*

"Oh, I know what you're going to say, Cordie. I can tell. But I know what I saw." There was a light in her eyes that had only flickered dimly since Mum had left, but today it was full, bright, and glowing. "I am so happy."

If Mum were here, she would have said something like, *You made your bed, Cordie, now you have to lie in it.* Mum was great with sayings like that. Except that Mum had made this bed, too, at least partially. She'd made it by leaving us in the first place.

I took a deep breath. And another. "Okay, well, we should probably get back home."

"Oh, no, not until I give this to Mr. Doyle. He wanted to

borrow it." She pulled *A Child's Book of Selkies* out of the diaper bag hanging on the back of the pram. "He was asking about this part—the part about the island."

I took the book from her and held it out of her reach. "No. Mr. Doyle is not borrowing this book."

Ione made a mad face and shouted, "He's my friend, Cordie!" The long-haired man looked over at us from the window inside Whale of a Tale. If she raised her voice any higher, Mr. Doyle would hear all the way down at his nasty little shop. Then I'd be outnumbered.

"We need to finish it first. You don't loan someone a book when you are right in the middle of it. Besides, it was Mum's favorite. Maybe she wouldn't want us to loan it out."

I'd made a good point, so Ione shrugged and rolled her eyes a tiny bit, which was her way of acknowledging that I was right without actually saying so. And then, as quickly as her bad mood had come, it was gone, floating away on the morning breeze that played with her pigtails. She'd done them herself, to look nice for Mum, I guessed. They were a little askew but at least her hair was out of her face. Mum had been fond of intricately braiding our hair, but that was before. Since then, Ione's hair had resembled a bramble.

But not today.

"Can we go and see her, then? See if she's still there?"

It was my turn to shrug. "Um . . . okay, I guess." We rose and I wheeled the pram, following Ione as she ran down to the edge of the pier.

I caught up with her in a few seconds and we stood side by side, in the exact spot where we'd dropped our tears into the blue. Three from Ione, three from me, and one tiny silver one that slid down Neevy's cheek and silently splashed upon the foam far below. As we scanned the waves, I was planning in my mind what I'd say when we didn't see anything. Would I make up some story about how selkies have tea parties at the bottom of the sea every day at precisely eleven-thirty, just to keep her happy? Or would I tell her that I'd lied, that Mr. Doyle was a liar, and that yes, Mum had left her family by choice? Would I finally end this before it went too far?

As I weighed the benefits of the fantasy against the risks of the truth, Ione began tugging on my arm.

"There she is! There!"

Neevy started kicking her legs and moving her arms wildly.

"I don't see anything," I said, unbuckling Neevy from the pram and holding her on my hip.

"There!" Ione pointed, jumping up and down.

"*I don't see*—" I began, but Ione interrupted me by taking my face in her hands and pointing it a little left of where I had been looking.

A large, silvery-black seal swam out in the bay.

"Mum!" Ione called.

The seal swam toward us.

"I told you, Cordelia Sullivan," said the gravelly voice of Mr. Doyle from right behind me. "I told you."

Coincidence

I COULDN'T REMEMBER THE LAST TIME I'd seen a seal in
the bay—and this wasn't even a pixie seal, the small, gray
ones that Da researched. The kind that used to be abun-
dant but had vanished. This was just a regular seal. True, it
was very large, but Da would say it was a coincidence, and
coincidences happen. If they didn't, then no one would have
invented a word for them, now would they?

"Ione, we have to go," I said, so calmly that it surprised me.

"Not until you let me have a look at that book. The one
with the map," said Mr. Doyle. He glanced quickly at me, at
the book that was still in Ione's hands, and then away, back
out at the seal. He kept shaking his head like he didn't believe it. "Look at her out there. Can't you see it? She's a
selkie all right, just look at her eyes."

The seal was too far away for us to see its eyes, but Ione
and Mr. Doyle were hypnotized by the animal just the
same.

"Come on, Ione." I pulled her arm, but she stood fast.

"She's so happy out there," Ione said with a sigh. "I can see why she wanted to go back."

Mr. Doyle finally turned away from the seal and bent down next to Ione and whispered. In less than a second, she handed him the book.

"But you can only look at it, you can't borrow it. Cordie says it's too special to loan out."

"I'll bet she does," Mr. Doyle muttered, flipping through the book to the page with the map. He stared at it for a moment, then flipped some more. "Is this it, then? The only page with a map?"

I didn't answer. Ione shrugged. "I don't know. You can read about it if you want, but the words are pretty boring."

"I just wanted to see the map," he said.

He turned each page, one by one, looking carefully at both sides. He grunted a couple of times. I was tempted to snatch the book away, but I was afraid it would rip.

I would just wait him out.

He was quickly becoming very exasperated.

"Oh," said Ione, pointing out to the bay. "I think she's gone. She hasn't come up in a while. She must have swum away for a bit."

I had been too busy watching Mr. Doyle paw through Mum's book to notice the vanishing seal. When Mr. Doyle's head snapped up to search for the sea, I retrieved the book. Gently, of course.

"We'll be going now," I announced, thrusting Neevy back in the carriage and buckling her in. "Now."

Ione took the book from me and thumbed through it herself. "I am sorry you didn't find what you were looking for, Mr. Doyle. Are you sure he can't borrow it, Cordie?" She was about to give me her begging face when Mr. Doyle himself interrupted.

"Don't need it. That's a fantasy map, not the real thing. I've been out there, in that patch of the water a thousand times over. There's no island there. No island, no treasure. A person would be a fool to look for it. It's not there." His shoulders slumped and he put his hands in his pockets. Right now he resembled a turtle more than a puffer fish.

"That's because it's magical," Ione retorted. "You have to believe to see it. Isn't that the way magic works?"

I was not about to waste the day debating the rules of magic with Mr. Doyle. Without another word, I pulled Ione along, down the streets of Selkie Bay, all the way back to our little house. We were out of breath when we got there, but I was not too tired to think about something that had really started to bother me.

"Can we go and see Mum in the morning?" Ione asked, interrupting my thoughts. We were inside now, and Ione was cutting bits of cheese for our sandwiches. She fed a little piece to Neevy, who gobbled it up. "I think she'd like that."

But I was barely listening. Instead I was trying to picture the island Mum had shown us, out between the two old guardian rocks. There had been a glimmer of an isle out there. I remembered it.

It was probably the same one Mr. Doyle said didn't exist.

But maybe it really did.

The Buried Treasure
of the Pirate Queen

I LOCKED ALL THE DOORS and checked the windows twice.
Secretly, of course. I didn't want to scare Ione.

But I was kind of scared myself.

I'd never been home at night in our house without Mum
or Da. And though yesterday I'd been sure I wouldn't be
afraid—that was yesterday.

"Can we stay up as late as we want?" Ione asked me, once
Neevy had fallen asleep. We'd scooted her crib into our
room, so that we'd all be together through the night. It'd
been Ione's idea, but I rather liked it.

"No."

She made a face, this time one involving a stuck-out tongue
and crossed eyes, but went back to playing with an old chess
set. Ione had given every piece a name and had built them a
castle from books. The pieces were celebrating the return of
the queen. Ione made them dance and sing—she played more
happily than I'd seen her do in months. I envied her.

But I had other things to do than eavesdrop on a chess-piece party. I pulled out A *Child's Book of Selkies* and began to read.

When in Seal form, the Selkie naturally prefers the sea, or one of the small islands that dot the coast. The most remarkable of these islands is called the Kingdom of the Selkies. It is the largest isle, and a place where Selkies can shed their skins (or not) at their leisure. Selkies are in no danger of being captured by Humans in the Kingdom. That is because the island is hidden and remains hidden to this day. Only those whom the Selkies trust know the details of sailing to this island. It is rumored that at certain times of day, the island is completely invisible, due to the position and glare of the sun.

If one were lucky enough to stumble upon the island, one would be fortunate, indeed. A simple dig or two might reveal hidden treasure, for selkies are fond of things that shine, like silver and gold. However, navigating to the isle is treacherous. The island is protected by formidable guardian rocks, sudden storms, and dense fog. Legends report many shipwrecks near the coast of the Kingdom.

Attempting to plunder the island would be a very poor idea, to be sure.

I didn't realize I'd been reading aloud until Ione stopped playing and asked, "What's *plunder* mean?"

"It means taking something that's not yours."

"Oh, like you did with that money." Was Ione ever going to stop annoying me about the money and where it came from?

"Do you really think I'm a thief? Or some kind of pirate?" I asked.

Ione played with the knight, drumming it against her knee as she thought. "I dunno, Cordie. Mum would be mad if you stole, but since she's a selkie now maybe she thinks about things differently." She cocked her head and looked up at me.

I wanted to scream at her, *Mum is not a selkie*, but yelling at Ione was never a good idea. So I just took a deep breath and looked back at the book, at the map of the island. I wasn't thinking of plundering it, but I did feel the urge to investigate. Especially since Mr. Doyle really seemed to *not* want us to. *No island, no treasure*, he'd said. And I probably would have thought it was just a bunch of nonsense except that Selkie Bay was not only known for its relationship with the mythical selkies. Another legend was the pirate queen's treasure, the same lady with all the pubs named after her.

But going off on the *Dreaming Lass* with my sisters probably wasn't a great plan.

"Cordie, we should go there! To the island. I bet Mum's there right now. That's where I'd go if I were a selkie. I'd go right to my own island. Please can we go?"

"No."

"Why not? Why can't we go? Is it because last time we went on the *Dreaming Lass* you turned green and tossed your guts overboard?"

"No."

"Then why?"

I wanted to tell her, *Because there will be no selkies on the island at all, because they aren't real.* But I knew she'd hate me for it, if she believed me, which she wouldn't. She probably just needed to see for herself.

Maybe it wasn't such a bad idea to pay a little visit to the selkies' island.

I sighed and quietly began to memorize every centimeter of the map.

"Please."

Reluctantly, I nodded. A trip to the island might be the very proof I needed to lay to rest Ione's *Mum is a selkie* fantasy—the magical island would be quite uninhabited. If we found it at all. It would be a harsh lesson, though. "Yes, I suppose we might try to find that island. We might find something else out there, too."

Ione stopped playing with her chess pieces and looked up at me. "What else is out there?"

"On the island of the selkies, the one they call the kingdom? Maybe lost treasure."

"We can find it, I bet. Mum tried to show it to us! And of course she'd know where it was, being a selkie and all." She knocked over one of the walls of her book castle in her excitement and didn't even notice. "But why do we need a treasure? Don't we have enough money from what you—?" Ione had scooted close to me on the floor and was now looking at the map intently.

"For the last time, I didn't steal that money. And there isn't that much of it, anyway," I said, even though my feet were sore from walking on it to the harbor and back. "But there might be so much more than that, out there on that island. They say a ship belonging to a pirate queen sank just outside of the bay, hundreds of years ago. They found the wreck but no gold. Maybe the captain stashed the treasure somewhere on an island."

"Do you think that's why Mr. Doyle wanted the map?" Ione asked.

"Maybe."

"He said it was a fake map. He said there was no island out there."

"But we know there is," I said. "Because Mum tried to show us."

Ione smiled and kissed the queen in her hand.

Into the Sea

I DIDN'T SLEEP MUCH THAT NIGHT. It didn't help that Da called to make sure we were being watched over by Maura and I had to lie to him that she was in the bathroom, so I felt kind of awful about it. It was a quick call, and his voice was strained. We both remembered the sugar jar and what was said. And what wasn't said. So when I tried to close my eyes, every little sound made me jump. When the house finally lit up with the day's sun, I might have slept for a few minutes.

I knew I would be yawning all day, but I didn't care.

Today was a day for adventuring and finding lost things.

* * *

"Cordie, come on!" Ione had run ahead and was standing a block away, impatient hands resting on her hips. Neevy was still asleep in the carriage. We'd raced out of the house early to get to the dock before anyone noticed. Sure, there were workers already there, down at the bad end, but the strip was nearly deserted. I shook my head at Ione, turned the pram, and went down a side street to the small outdoor market that opened early in the morning during the summer. Different folks set up their tables on different days, depending on what they had to sell. By August, so many booths would be packed into the little street, it would be hard to walk. But on this quiet morning, early risers such as the Sullivan sisters were bound to stand out if they weren't careful. Slowly, trying hard not to draw too much attention, I wheeled ahead.

Ione ran into me, nearly knocking me over. "Cordie, what are you doing?"

"I am getting us something to eat," I said. "And keep your voice down. I don't want nosy Mr. Doyle to know what we are up to."

Ione was usually hungry, so she seemed satisfied with my answer. I hated using Mum's money from the jar, the money that should have gone to the rent, but if we found a treasure, we'd have more than enough.

Ione spied some fruit-filled pies that looked like heaven. We bought two and quickly ate them before Neevy woke. I felt a little bad, but she wouldn't have liked the tartness of the berries, and besides, in a minute I would find something that was more suitable for a baby.

I just needed to think.

Ione worked her way over to a man selling fried chips from a van. "No, Ione," I said. "We have to be smart about this. We can't spend all the money right now."

I surveyed the market. *What wouldn't spoil quickly?* Ione was surveying, too, no doubt looking for the tastiest snack or the cake with the most frosting.

I chose some apples and some slightly green bananas.

"Those aren't ripe yet," Ione said.

"I know."

There was a loaf of really hard bread, like Da said they have in France. It looked sturdy enough.

There was some goat cheese coated in wax that caught my eye. "Do you need to keep this in the fridge?" I asked the man, who had a goatlike face to match his cheese.

"Not so long as you don't let it get too hot. Keep it cool, and dry."

A lady had a case of water bottles. I bought ten.

"Why do we need so many?" Ione chirped.

"If we don't bring our own water, what are we supposed to drink?" I supposed that's what you did when you were eight—forgot about all the problems of day-to-day living. However, I was eleven, nearly twelve. I couldn't afford the luxury of forgetfulness.

I stuffed as many of our bags as I could underneath the pram next to the three life vests we'd brought from home and pushed us along, back toward the harbor.

Near the end of the dock, bobbing among several other dinghies, was the *Dreaming Lass*.

Even though we'd been out in it only a few months ago, it was smaller than I remembered.

"Oh, Cordie, this is going to be fun!" Ione jumped up and down. "I hope we packed enough diapers in Neevy's diaper bag." Ione looked inside to check, then pulled out one of the hand shovels we used when we weeded the blackberry bramble behind the house. "Well, this explains why it's so heavy." She was about to put it back inside, next to the other digging tools I'd found, when she froze, the shovel poised in midair.

"Cordie," she whispered, turning my attention from the boat to the long shadow that stretched from about two feet in front of us all the way to the edge of the *Dreaming Lass*.

"And where do you think you are going?" said Mr. Doyle. His voice first thing in the morning was even more scratchy than usual.

"Nowhere," I said, before Ione could butt in. "Not that it's any of your business. We don't work for you anymore. Remember?"

He took in the shovel, the *Dreaming Lass*, and the old book sticking out of the diaper bag and said, "You'll never find it, you know."

He crossed his arms in front of his chest and stood there, glaring at me, the same way he'd stood and glared at Mum that foggy morning on the beach when she'd last taken us out in the boat.

I didn't say anything. Ione didn't either, but as she tried to stuff the shovel back in the bag, she fumbled a bit and it clanked to the ground.

Mr. Doyle was there in a blink, picking up the shovel and stuffing it in the bag for us, then zipping the whole thing closed. "Good to see you are going prepared at least." He patted the bag. Then he eyed us more closely, with squinty eyes. "I can't imagine your da is happy about this. Never seemed to like the sea, that one. Didn't like it when your mum took you out, as I recall."

I looked at Ione to silence her. She put both hands over her mouth to try to keep her words inside. *Very discreet, my sister.*

"Oh, he doesn't know, does he?"

I willed Ione to keep her mouth shut, but she kept looking at me with a look on her face that fairly screamed, *He's figured out our secret, Cordie!*

"Maybe I should go and tell him? What do you think about that, Cordelia Sullivan?"

"Go ahead," I said bravely.

"Yeah. Go ahead and try. You won't find him, though, because he's gone." Ione was quite pleased with herself.

"Just stop talking, Ione. It's none of his business."

"Listen to the way you talk. Just a day or so ago, you were begging me for work. And now look at you, full of spit and fire. That's no way to treat an elder." Mr. Doyle scowled and shook both his head and his finger at me.

Taking a young girl out on a boat to trick the tourists into thinking she is a selkie girl, to boost your own business, is no way to treat a kid, either. But I didn't have time to argue with Mr. Doyle. Neevy was starting to fuss, so I turned my attention to her, trying to ignore the cranky old man, just like Mum had ignored him.

"And if your da's gone and left you, too, well I suppose that makes you abandoned. There's authorities that can take care of that. Perhaps I should make a call."

I didn't say anything else. Not one word. I just turned around and started pushing that pram away from Mr. Doyle and away from our boat. Not fast, because I didn't want him to know he scared me, even though he did. Ione was right there beside me. For a second, we were an unstoppable force, the Sullivan sisters, off to find our fortune.

Ione finally chanced a glance back. "He's gone," she said.

We turned around, raced to the *Dreaming Lass*.

My hands started to get clammy. I didn't know much about piloting the boat by myself, but Mum had showed both Ione and me the basics. I could manage to start the small motor and get us away from here. I was pretty sure I could, anyway. But still, I had doubts. What kind of big sister takes her little sisters out in a boat without telling anyone? It sounded crazy. It sounded like something I should not even consider doing.

It sounded exactly like something Mum would have done.

"Help me, Ione. We've got to get the cover off this thing."

Dropping the bread bag with a thud, Ione skipped over and drew the boat close by the painter. I reached down to loosen the cover and pull it off from one side, then the other. The boat was filled with water halfway up the sides. The cover hadn't done its job. I wished Neevy were old enough to help us.

I surveyed the dock. Still empty. Mr. Doyle was nowhere to be seen.

"There, Cordie, look there!" Ione pointed out to sea, her voice giddy and squealy.

I looked, but I didn't see anything.

"Is someone coming?" My stomach seized up, just like it did when I got seasick, and I wasn't even in the boat yet.

"She's coming, Cordie! I knew she would!"

Ione pointed out to the gray morning sea. The sun was rising slowly in the east, reflecting upon the waves like molten silver.

"There!" And she pointed again.

Through the white foam that frosted the waves, up popped the black face of the seal.

Follow the Leader

IT TOOK US ABOUT FIFTEEN MINUTES of bailing to empty the boat. And finally, with the help of one of the Patel boys, who was on his way to work at Chippy's, we got the small outboard running.

"Where are you going, anyway?" he asked. I shrugged. The Patel boys were twins, Niall and Raj, and I could never tell them apart, even though both of them had been in my class this year. They swapped identities all the time—drove the headmistress crazy.

Ione cheered as the motor warmed up, and I wanted to cheer, too, but I stayed quiet. I was still too busy looking from side to side, watching to see if anyone was paying attention to the poor Sullivan girls as they struggled with their crummy-looking boat.

"So it's a secret, then?" Niall or Raj asked. "Where's your father? Isn't he going with you?"

I shrugged again.

"You're brave, Cordie," Niall or Raj said. "So which one am I, Raj or Niall?"

"Niall."

"Ha! It's Raj."

I reminded him that he probably had to work, which he did. So he left.

"Thanks, Raj," I called after him.

"Ha! It's Niall," he shouted back.

I felt bad leaving Neevy's pram behind, but even folded up, it wouldn't fit well into the boat. And if we had treasure to bring back, we'd have to have room for it. Hopefully, the carriage would still be there when we got back. I let myself picture it for a minute—us returning triumphantly to Selkie Bay, loaded with treasure, pram waiting to be filled with Neevy and gold, as we made our way home to Da.

My head knew it wasn't really possible. That almost-twelve-year-old girls and their little sisters weren't the kinds of folks that found hidden treasure. But my heart wanted to try. And trying something felt so much better than sitting around feeling numb. I guessed Ione wasn't the only one with make-believe dreams. But which was crazier? Finding buried treasure or having a seal for a mum?

At least treasure could solve some of our problems.

Maybe not all of them, but some of them. And if we didn't find treasure, because we didn't find an island and therefore didn't find selkies, well, that would solve a problem, too. The Ione problem.

The sun was rising higher, the silver glow atop the water deepening to gold. Even the seal, whose head was still sitting perkily above the water, seemed cast from bronze.

So this was it, then. I was really going to do it.

Where exactly did I think I was going to go?

The minute we'd plopped Neevy and all our stuff into the boat, the wind picked up.

"Put this on," I said, handing Ione a life vest. I put on mine and strapped the extra-small one on Neevy.

"Onward!" I commanded to Ione, and adjusted the choke. The engine stalled.

"Oh no, captain!" she cried.

I stood up, gained my balance, and pulled the starter cord.

It took a few times of pulling with all my might, but eventually, the *Dreaming Lass* sputtered back to life. I sat and used the rusty handle to steer.

We left the harbor within a few minutes. I was thrilled. Not a soul was out with their boat this early, except for the fisherfolk—but most of them had left before dawn and were far off the coast by now, and the ones that were on the other side of the harbor were too busy checking their nets and cages to worry about a little dinghy. The morning moon hung above our heads like a pearl in the sky, lovely and hopeful. We could not have been luckier.

But luck is funny that way. The minute you think you've got it all figured out, luck can change, faster than the blink of an eye or the gust of a wild wind.

Or the thick hand of fog.

That's what it's like sometimes, when fog grabs you. It's like a giant's hand, and often you manage to slip through its fingers for a while, but then it reaches out and takes you again.

We'd been flitting in and out, around and between the foggy fingers for about thirty minutes when it finally surrounded and completely enveloped us.

I shut the motor off.

"Which way are we supposed to go, Cordie?" Ione looked behind us, to where the coast should have been. Instead, we could see only misty white.

I could hear the fear in Ione's voice. "Cordie? You do know where we are going, right?"

There was no quick lie that came to me, so I just nodded and looked off.

The sky over the sea was a beautiful thing—white with fog, except for a small circle where the moon watched over us. Or it would have been beautiful if I hadn't been so scared I thought I might pee myself. "Uh, Ione . . ." I started.

What was I going to say? I am an idiot for taking you and Neevy on the boat? I don't really know where to go.

"Oh there you are again!" said Ione, switching from scared to joyful in but a second. She pointed over the edge of the *Dreaming Lass.* "It's Mum," she whispered.

The seal had popped up again, timidly inching closer.

"No one followed us, Mum. It's okay," Ione said gently,

then turned to me. "When she's her seal-self, she's not quite like a person, more like an animal."

"What makes you think you know so much about selkies?" I asked.

"Well, I read the book you gave me. Some of the words were big and old, so I had to guess about them. And it is in our blood, after all. Isn't that what you said when you told me about Mum?"

"Sure."

A wave splashed against our small boat, giving me a mouthful of salty water. I spat it out and wiped my face with the back of my hand. Ione laughed.

Neevy woke with a whimper that quickly morphed into a full-fledged howling session. The seal turned its head this way and that, obviously not liking the noise.

"It's okay, Mum, she's just got a wet diaper," Ione said to the seal. "Cordie will change her now. Don't worry." Turning to me she said, "She doesn't like to hear her baby cry. Come on, hurry up. Change her."

Changing a squirrelly baby in a life vest on a bobbing boat is not the easiest thing to do. With the taste of salt in my mouth, the smell of the diaper, and the roll of the waves under the boat, I was pretty sure I was going to puke. Just like Da.

"You look like a ghost, Cordie. A pale ghost."

"Well, I am not a ghost because ghosts don't vomit." I lay

back in the *Dreaming Lass*, trying to focus on the moon instead of the shifting boards under my back.

"It's okay. The map is around here somewhere. Maybe I can find the island."

"Yeah, right." I hoped Ione would just shut up and let us drift for a minute until my stomach settled. Then I'd get us moving again. "Let's not start the motor up just yet. I need a few minutes."

I must have felt really nauseated because I closed my eyes and the next thing I knew, Neevy was snuggled up next to me and Ione's voice, soft as the breeze, was floating around us.

Ione's Tale

Once there were three special princesses. They were special because they didn't even know they were princesses. But they were. And they were also special because they were selkie princesses. But they didn't know that, either. And that was okay.

Sometimes people don't know everything that they think they know.

These princesses were trying to find a treasure.

And their mum. They were trying to find their mum, too.

Their mum was a selkie, of course. And she'd been called back to the sea, but she never really left them. Not at all. She loved her three princesses too much to ever be far from them. So she stayed in the bay, hoping her daughters would one day see her and know who she was.

It was the middle princess, the bravest one, who noticed that the seal in the bay was their mum. The biggest princess didn't understand because she was too busy being angry at her mother for being a selkie, and mad at her da, too, even though no one was quite sure why.

She was just busy being mean. A lot. And she didn't used to be mean. Not all the time, anyway. And the baby princess spent most of her time eating bananas and pooping, so she wasn't much for noticing important things like mums disguised as seals.

So the princesses followed their mother selkie to the ocean, where she had been watching over them from the edge of the sea. Selkies will do anything for their pups because they love them so much, so their mum stayed as a seal and swam next to their boat, leading the way to the secret island.

You are probably thinking they were searching for treasure, and you would be right, but not at first. At first they had to find their seal coats. They didn't have any yet because they had been born on land. That's just the way it was.

They had to get to the Kingdom of the Selkies quickly, because they were racing an old man with a puffer-fish head. He had special powers called the Authorities and he had threatened to use them on the princesses. He wanted the treasure, too.

Really, everybody wants treasure. Except for maybe ants. Ants don't want treasure. Ants like sugar.

Anyway, even though it was scary, the seal mother guided her pups in the boat through the dangerous waters. She nudged the boat this way and that, in between the two gigantic rocks, and through the secret water passage to the Kingdom of the Selkies.

When they finally got there, they met the rest of the selkie family. They had all kinds of uncles and aunts and cousins. At first, everyone was a little shy, but it didn't take long for all the seals to adore the three princesses. That's the thing about being a princess. You get adored a lot. And, the best part was, the sisters each got to pick out a seal coat. Even though the middle princess wanted a purple one, she knew that her mother would say no, for even selkie mums have to say no sometimes. So they picked out coats of soft, shiny fur and their mum helped them learn the ways of the selkies.

Of all the things they learned about the selkies, the most important was to always stay together.

The Fog

IONE WASN'T TALKING ANYMORE. I sat up, careful not to nudge Neevy. She'd seemed cozy cuddled next to me at first, but it didn't take long for her warmth to turn to heat.

The heat was familiar and fevery.

"Oh no," I muttered. Our grand voyage to the island was going from poorly planned to insanely stupid.

"Don't you feel it, Cordie?" Ione whispered.

"I don't feel anything," I said.

"That's what I am talking about. The nothing. The ocean isn't supposed to feel like nothing."

She was right. The ocean was so, so very calm. Once, when Neevy was a newborn and lay sleeping quietly, Mum had said, "Just watch, Cordie, this is the calm before the storm." Mum had been paler than usual, her eyes not as dark and bright. She said it was the birth of the baby that always took it out of her. She didn't look like herself at all. But she had been right. Soon after the calm, Neevy exploded into loud cries of hunger.

But now there was no explosive storm, no howling winds that surrounded us, just the silent sea and an eerie blanket of white so thick I could barely see Ione sitting across from me.

"Where's Mum?" Ione asked.

"How should I know?" It took me a moment to realize she was talking about the seal again, of course. But just like the real Mum, the seal was nowhere in sight.

"I'm scared, Cordie. This is creepy. Start the boat. Let's go."

"And where would we go? I can't see a thing, Ione! How am I supposed to tell which way to go? What if I go the wrong direction and we get lost at sea and never come home? How would you feel about that?"

If you are guessing that Ione burst into tears at this point, you are right. I shouldn't have said what I did, and I shouldn't have said it in a mean voice. Neevy started fussing and I had to hold her and rock her, without rocking the boat much.

"What about Mum? Will she be safe out there?" Ione sobbed, wiping her eyes with the back of her sleeve, searching the surrounding cloud of white for the silvery-black head of the seal.

I wanted to reach out and hold her, too. But I was afraid

to loosen my grip on Neevy. Ione leaned far, far over the edge, straining to find the seal.

"Sit down now!" I yelled.

"But she's right there!" She reached with one arm, out toward where that seal swam, a few meters away from us.

"Why doesn't she come closer? Does she need our help? We have to help her!" she cried.

"That seal doesn't need our help! It's a seal, for crying out loud!" If anyone needed help, it was us—three girls in a boat in the fog, drifting to nowhere. I grabbed hold of the rusty handle, wondering if I should risk starting the motor again. What if I rammed us into a rock? Or another boat?

Please tell me which way to go. I didn't know if I was begging God or that seal. It really didn't matter, as long as one of them did something. But I couldn't see God, and that seal just stayed right next to us.

"Keep us safe, Mum," Ione called out. Her earlier bravery had melted away, leaving only sobs.

I'd about had it with Ione and her stupid seal. And the way she could just believe something so easily. Gullible. That's what people who believe anything are called. Here we were lost in the middle of the ocean and there she was, talking to the seal.

So I was going to let it all out and just yell at her, at how stupid this was, and how stupid *she* was, but then, just after I called *Ione* in my harshest tone, that seal turned and

122

barked at me. It barked like a dog only much, much louder. So loud that Ione stopped crying for a moment and got that look on her face like she did when I'd gotten in trouble with Mum. Her eyes opened wide and she said, "Mum's mad at you, Cordie."

And I know it sounds crazy, but when I looked over at the seal, she was looking right back at me with her unblinking black eyes.

"No, Ione, she is *not* mad at me," I said calmly, the moist fog tasting salty on my tongue.

At least I hoped she wasn't..

Castle on the Sea

"FOLLOW HER. Follow Mum," Ione said.

I was about to refuse, even though I myself still had no idea which way to go, when the fog thinned a little and I saw the two large guardian rocks Mum had told us about. Ione saw them, too.

"Through those rocks, Cordie. We just have to follow Mum through the rocks and then we'll be able to see the island! We didn't even need the map!"

I felt a tickle of excitement in my belly. I pulled the starter and the *Dreaming Lass* came alive once more.

"Oh, I'm so proud of us! Aren't you proud of us, Mum?" Ione waited for the seal to answer, which of course she didn't. "Quick, Cordie. Let's go!"

The seal was a few meters in front of us now, and I didn't want to hit her with the boat.

"Move, seal! Get out of the way!" I cried.

Ione gave me a surprised shove. "Cordie, that was rude. You didn't even say *please*. Mum would be shocked at your bad manners. Besides, look, she's stopped and waiting for us. She wants us to follow."

It was as if the seal looked over her shoulder. *Hurry up! Come on!*

"Hold on to Neevy while I steer."

Following the bobbing silver head of the seal, I motored us onward, hoping with all my heart that we'd make it to the island. It didn't have to be magical or anything, it didn't even have to have treasure, it just needed to have a shore and I'd be happy.

Between the rugged guardians we putted, the fog now only wisps of mist that made everything look mystical, which made me wonder if that's where the word came from. Then the island appeared, as if the sea were the sky and the land was rising from the clouds. Tall, spindly spires glistened, and giant stones of unusual shapes became clearer.

"It looks like a castle!" Ione cried.

In a way, she was right. If a castle had ever been built by a bunch of seals, it probably would have looked like this. Tumbly, raggedy, jumbled.

But still. There it was. We had found it.

I was so happy, so focused on the strange castle in front of me that I did not notice the upcoming reef. The boat jerked, followed by the most horrible scraping noise.

A wave came and rammed the *Dreaming Lass* against the rocks. Hard.

"Geez, Cordie! A little warning would have been nice. I almost dropped Neevy."

I tried not to panic. Dropping Neevy would have been the least of our problems. The fact was, the *Dreaming Lass* was now taking on water and I didn't know how much longer we could stay afloat.

"Ione, I don't want you to get scared, but I think we might have to swim for it. You're going to have to be brave."

"I'm not the one afraid of the water, Cordie."

I glared, though she wasn't looking at me any longer. And I wasn't afraid of the water. Water didn't make me barf. Waves made me barf. There was a difference.

"I'm going to try to get us as close as I can. But if the boat flips, hold on to the diaper bag. It has our food in it and we are going to need it. I'll hold Neevy and swim with her. And don't take off the life vest whatever you do."

Ione nodded. The whites of her eyes were huge. For all of her brave talk, she was terrified again.

"Mum, keep us safe," she whispered to the seal we could no longer see.

Yeah, Mum, don't let us drown.

The water was around our ankles in the boat when the motor gurgled to a stop. I saw the shadowy spires of the island growing bigger and bigger before I realized that although the motor had stopped, the boat itself had not.

"Cordie, look! Mum's helping!" Ione pointed behind us.

There was the seal, her nose to the left of the outboard motor, nudging our little boat along.

And I didn't know what to say, so I didn't say anything at all. I just stared with my mouth open like an idiot.

"Don't make her do all the work," I said finally. "Help paddle!"

I reached beneath the seat to where two emergency oars were stowed. We paddled hard.

But despite our efforts, the *Dreaming Lass* sank just off the coast of the selkies' isle.

So we swam. Sort of. Once in the water, I could feel a solidness under my feet. "Just a little more, Ione, and you'll feel the bottom, too." I held Neevy as far out of the water as I could manage. To the right of me, Ione dog-paddled, still holding the diaper bag until she, too, felt the sand beneath her shoes.

Neevy, who had been an angel through most of the trip, decided that since we were approaching land, she should have a nice, fat fit. But I didn't even care. No doubt she was hungry. We all were. I thought of the bread in the diaper bag, which would probably be soggy, and the cheese. Ugh, the cheese. My stomach started to growl, anyway.

The fog was still patchy and I could see the seal leading the way to a grayish beach, surrounded by tall rocks.

The seal turned and barked something.

It was a strange welcome to the Kingdom of the Selkies.

Reunion

THE ISLAND WAS SMALLER THAN I thought it would be.

I could see how ships might have crashed against it, for it was like one moment it wasn't there, and the next it was. All around, except for the beach, the edges of rocks jutted out menacingly.

And it was quiet, but for the sea.

The beaches around Selkie Bay were rarely quiet during the season. They were loud with tourists, or noisy with seabirds squawking from the sky, claiming fish and trash from the water below.

But there were no sounds here on the island. Nothing except the sound of a baby screeching as her eight-year-old sister laid her on the sand and started to replace her wet dirty diaper with a wet clean one. And then there was the sound of the eight-year-old saying things she knew better than to say as she tried to get wet diaper tape to stick to a wet diaper. Also, there was the sound of me, combing through the diaper bag in search of an apple.

And nearby was the heavy, uneven breathing of the large black seal.

Ione carried Neevy over to me as I searched through our soggy things. In addition to damp diapers, we had some pretty beat-up bananas and a loaf of limp bread. The cheese was okay, and the water bottles were, too. Inside a zippered pocket was the sugar-jar money—sopping wet, but at least it wasn't at the bottom of the sea. As I took the shovels from the diaper bag, I found what I was looking for—the apples. I raised one high into the air in victory. At the sight of it, Neevy threw her arms around excitedly. At home, we called it the cookie dance. But since we didn't have cookies, Neevy would have to settle for apple. Pre-chewed apple. It might sound gross, and I felt like a mother bird, feeding chewed-up food to a baby, but she had to be fed and that was that.

Luckily, she seemed not to mind as I placed bits of mushed-up apple in her hand so she could put them in her mouth. Only once was the chunk too big and not chewed-up enough, but she quickly coughed it out.

"Don't you want an apple, Ione?" She must have been starving, too. Ione was always hungry. "Ione?" I called again when she didn't answer.

I turned around in time to see her kneel down over by where the silver-black seal had beached itself, midway up the shore. I could see her skinny legs trembling.

"Step back, Ione," I whispered. "I think we should leave it alone for now."

"It's not an *it*. It's a *she*. And *she* is Mum," she whispered back. "And Mum is hurt. Right here." She pointed to a spot between her chest and her left shoulder.

I looked past Ione to the seal's middle as it rose and fell. I didn't know how fast a seal was supposed to breathe, but the rhythm seemed kind of slow. But then, seals were used to holding their breath, so maybe this was normal.

But what wasn't normal was how this seal had showed up at the dock. Or how she had stayed with us during the fog. Or how she had used her nose to nudge us here—to the island of the selkies.

No, none of that was normal at all.

"Cordie," Ione said, walking back toward me. "I think you should go and look at her. You're the oldest. She needs *you*."

Ione, for all of her conviction about Mum being a seal, was scared and I knew it. It's one thing to think your mother has turned into a seal. It's quite another to be stranded with your seal-mum on an isle with no other grownups around.

I was scared, too.

But I knew it would be worse if I showed Ione my fear. And though Neevy was still only a baby, she could smell fear, I was sure. Probably all babies can smell fear. The last thing I needed was a double little-sister freak-out.

"Well, if you come and keep Neevy happy, I'll take a look at . . . her."

Quickly, Ione skipped over to me and took Neevy from my arms.

"Now, take this and see if you can get Neevy to drink some water." I handed Ione a bottle.

I started toward the seal. I didn't want to frighten it or have it jump at me or anything, so I thought it would be a good idea to talk to it as I walked.

"Um . . . seal? Hello there, seal."

"Her name is *Mum!*" called Ione. Upon hearing the word *Mum*, the seal turned its head around and looked at me.

"See?" *Smug, smug Ione.*

"Okay, *Mum,*" I began, still taking quiet steps toward where the seal lay. "I'd like to take a look at your, um, shoulder, I think that's what you call it. I am not going to hurt you."

"She knows that. She's your mum."

I was almost right next to her now. She watched my every move with her dark eyes. I had my hands out in front of me as if to say, *It's going to be all right.* She didn't even blink. So I knelt down and touched her gently with one hand.

She was soft, perhaps the softest thing I had ever touched. Softer than the coat that once hung in our closet. Maybe even softer than a cloud. I put the other hand on her and started rubbing her, as if she were a dog. She seemed to like it and rolled toward me.

The slash on her shoulder was horrible. I gasped when I saw it close up, but still she didn't turn away. Had she gotten it from the rusted propeller as she nudged us along? I had no idea how she swam with us and pushed us to the shore with an injury like that. It looked like the kind of wound that could kill.

"That cut looks disgusting," said Ione, scuffling toward me with Neevy in her arms. "But don't worry, Mum, we are going to fix you up." Ione knelt down on the other side of the seal, her good side, and put Neevy right up next to her.

"Ione, what are you doing?" I whispered, trying not to scare the seal.

"Mum would want to hold her, don't you think? She hasn't seen her in a long time." Ione then gently put both of her arms around the seal and buried her face in the soft, smooth fur. "I missed you so much, Mum. I know you had to go. But I missed you so much. We all did."

I wiped my eyes with the backs of my hands, then my runny nose with my sleeve. "Ione, you ought to step back from . . . Mum. Remember how you said that when she is in her seal form, she's more animal-like? Well, you don't want to spook her. Besides, she's tired and needs to sleep."

And the seal did look tired. So tired. She gave what sounded like a sigh and closed her eyes.

I am going to find a way to help you, I promised her.

A lump rose in my throat and I tried to swallow it but it wouldn't go away.

I missed you, too, Mum.

Cousins of the Sea

WE SET UP A SMALL CAMP, there on the beach, next to the seal. The *Dreaming Lass* had washed up on the shore a few hours after we did. The leak in the boat wasn't near as bad as I had feared; it was tiny, in fact, but big enough to let in too much water, obviously. I'd watched Da repair enough boats to know what to do. I just needed to find the right materials. For now, we set it on its side as a windbreak, which was a good thing, because at the first gust of wind, all the money I'd laid out to dry almost blew away. This time, I placed each bill behind the windbreak, under a piece of shell. Once it was dry, I'd put it back in the diaper bag. Of course, that had to dry out, too.

The seal watched us as we placed our belongings around us, but she did not get up. She just lay there. A few steps from the beach, there were rocks and caves we were dying to explore, as well as those tall, spindly things, but we just couldn't leave her there, all alone.

"I thought it would be more like a castle. Close up, it just looks weird. Don't all kingdoms have castles?" Ione asked. I was out of lies, so I let her words float away to the clouds and put her on Neevy-patrol. Neevy was quite the crawler this afternoon, having given up carpet-swimming for fast, stomach-based land travel. "Just make sure she doesn't go toward the waves."

"Mum would never let her do such a thing, would you, Mum?" said Ione.

There was a small bark from the seal and Ione smirked.

Maybe it would be easier if I let myself believe the magic of it all. Yes. *Our mum is a selkie who is now stuck as a seal.* But I couldn't believe it. Stuff like that didn't really happen. I knew better.

"Still, Ione, watch her, okay?"

I didn't even wait for the eye roll, but turned my attention back to the seal. She probably needed to eat. I rummaged through our bag. There wasn't anything I thought a seal would like, but even if there was, I needed to save it for Neevy and Ione. And me, too. They'd never manage if I died of starvation on the first day.

"Okay, seal, let's see about getting you some fish. That's what you eat, right?" The seal remained uninterested in anything I said. "Oh, come on! You need to eat. You need to go and catch yourself some dinner." Before I realized how stupid I looked, I found myself pretending to swim down the beach to the waves. "The fish are there! In the ocean! And they are nummy, nummy, nummy!" I pretended to eat an imaginary fish.

The seal was unimpressed.

I changed my plan. It was probably okay to let her rest there. After all, she had to be tired after pushing us. But then I looked at the gash again and felt the worries rise. *What if the seal died here on the beach?*

Ione would lose her mind.

However, if I got her into the ocean, and then the *unexpected* happened . . . at least Ione wouldn't know. And maybe salty seawater would be good for the wound and help it heal.

"Come on, seal!" I called.

No response.

"Mum?" I called, just to see if it made any difference.

It did. Within seconds, the seal had scampered down the beach, favoring her left side, and was now bobbing happily, if a little weakly, in the water.

Ione came tearing across the beach, Neevy bouncing with laughter on her hip. "What are you doing? Where is Mum going? How could you let her go?" she shouted.

"She needs to eat. Seals eat fish, not apples."

"Yes, of course. I knew that," Ione said.

"So while she is gone, we should explore a bit, don't you think?"

"Only if you take this gigantic lug. I swear she's gained a hundred pounds since we left."

Ione struggled dramatically as she handed me the "gigantic lug," who was covered in sand but very smiley. I heaved Neevy up in my arms and we walked up the beach, past an outcropping of black rocks, to a series of caves.

"Be careful," I called to Ione, who ran ahead and disappeared within seconds.

The first cave was large and roomy. I didn't have to duck at all except to get inside. There were two others that were smaller. And all around the black, jagged rocks grew tangles of dark-leaved bushes.

"Looks like a house. A selkie house. This is much better than a castle!" Ione cried, clapping her hands. "This will be the family room, that is our room over there, and Mum can have her own room here."

"And the kitchen?" I asked absently as I reached down to check out the familiar-looking bramble. I was right, just like at home. Blackberries, and in full bloom, too. I felt a little better, knowing there was at least one source of food on this island.

"The kitchen is on the beach, of course. Easier to wash dishes that way," Ione said, running back to the beach carrying imaginary dishes.

I didn't bother to remind her that we didn't have any *real* dishes to wash. At least we had found shelter. And I had to admit, I was getting really tired. I yawned big and wide. Neevy did the same.

I sat down in the middle of the "family room" and let Neevy explore. It was funny how just a few weeks ago she was barely crawling, and now there was no stopping her.

Babies grow fast.

And Mum had missed a lot of Neevy's life, considering Neevy hadn't had much of a life so far.

Of all of us, Neevy had Mum's smile. They both had a dimple on the right that made every smile seem so sweet. But when I tried to remember the last time I saw Mum smile, all I could come up with was that day on the boat, when she'd tried to show us this very island. Otherwise, my last memories of her seemed small, and her face was always pale. And her hands were thin. I asked her once how she felt because it looked like the sort of question that needed asking.

"I am fine, Cordie. You don't need to worry. Sometimes it takes a person a while to get her strength back after having a baby."

But other kids' mums didn't look so weak for months after they had babies.

I rubbed my hand on Neevy's still-bald head. It was just as soft as the seal's fur. In the distance, I could see Ione kicking in the waves, dancing about like she didn't have a care. It must be nice not to worry about everything, like money, Mum, and Mr. Doyle calling the authorities about Da.

Da.

He was going to be really mad. But I just couldn't think about it now. I was tired of having to be Cordie-Solve-It-All *all the time.*

I just wanted to run around on the beach like Ione, kicking at the foam, jumping up and down excitedly.

"Cordie! Come quick!"

So I gathered up Neevy and ran to the waves, ready to do my share of kicking and jumping when I saw the head of the seal, bobbing along toward the beach.

"Mum's back," I said.

"But she's not alone! Look, Cordie! She brought pups! She brought our cousins!"

And there, trailing behind the black seal, were the silver-gray heads of about a dozen smaller seals.

"What?"

"Baby selkie cousins!"

I wanted to call for Ione to stand back. Seals were wild animals, after all. But I found myself just standing there. No words came out of my mouth. The large seal waddled over to me, let out a sigh, and lay at my feet, closing her eyes like she was very, very tired. The wound didn't look any better, but at least it didn't look worse.

All around her were seals of different sizes, most of them much smaller than her. None of them were dark or black. Their coats were a shimmery sort of gray. I'd never seen anything like them, except they looked a little like Da's pictures of pixie seals. Except that pixie seals had basically vanished, so it couldn't be them. They scampered up the beach and found places on the sand or on rocks and just sort of lay there, like they were taking a mid-afternoon nap.

"Oh, look at your little cousin, Neevy. Isn't he cute?"

I turned around to see Ione trying to carry the smallest seal in her arms, as if it were a baby. He was too big and heavy, though. But Ione was relentless.

"Ione, you better put that seal down before his mum sees you and bites you in the behind."

"Look at him. He is adorable. I am calling him Henry. Hello, Cousin Henry."

Remarkably, the bigger seals didn't seem to mind that Ione was attempting to pick up their babies, looking them in the eyes, and giving each of them a name. There ended up being fifteen of them altogether.

"Oh, Cordie, did you bring something to write on? Maybe we could use that selkie book and write their names in there; otherwise, I am just going to mix them up all the time. Are you really just going to stand around?"

The large black seal at my feet sighed in the way that I was getting used to. *Fine*, I thought, *I'll get the book from the diaper bag*. But the book was gone. And it hadn't been there when I went through our things earlier. Now it was probably lying at the bottom of the sea.

"Just tell me their names. I'll help you remember."

Ione looked at each one carefully before settling on a name. "Betty, Daisy, William, Kate, Brian, Finn, Sorcha, Fergal, Diana, Charlie, Mo, Dearbla, Michael, and Oisin."

"That's a strange collection of names," I said.

"I can't help it if that's what they look like. They are a strange collection of selkies."

"Maybe they already have names. Did you consider that? And what if they are just seals, Ione? Just seals."

But she wasn't listening to me. She was having a quiet conversation with little Henry, telling him that she was ready to choose her sealskin and trying to convince him that it was quite all right to change into a human any time he felt like it and that she'd turn her head away if he was at all worried about not having any clothes.

Wounded

THE BLACK SEAL was getting worse.

All through the evening, the small seals basked on the beach or frolicked in the waves hunting for fish, but not once did the bigger seal go into the sea. She repositioned herself a few times, but that was it. Even as night fell, she did not move. There was no chance of us going home tonight—not with the darkness and not with the ruined boat, so Ione and I decided to sleep with Neevy in the largest cave, and a few of the seals followed, but not the large one. She stayed on the beach. I lay so I could watch her in the moonlight. She was there when I fell asleep.

She was there every time I awoke throughout the night, which was about a hundred times.

* * *

In the morning, a soft blanket of gray fog hung over the Kingdom of the Selkies, making the sun a small white circle above the horizon. The sea was smooth in places, like dark glass, but rough and foamy in others. It was beautiful, but not a friendly-looking sea today. Not at all.

On the beach, however, the scene was all business, with Ione moving about like a little general in charge of the world.

"I'll make breakfast," said Ione. She quickly gathered some blackberries and fished out the goat cheese from the diaper bag. It was the same thing we'd had for dinner last night, but we didn't care. We were hungry. We'd decided to save the apples for Neevy, at least some of them. And luckily, she didn't seem to mind eating wet, mushed-up bread and brown bananas. I felt a little bad feeding it to her, since it looked so awful, but she needed to eat and the blackberries were too tart for her little tongue.

"No, none for you," Ione scolded Henry as he sniffed around our picnic. "You have to eat fish. There isn't enough for you. Go catch something. Shoo."

Like a puppy following commands, Henry scampered down the beach, approached the big seal, and sniffed at her a few times. She barked at him, so he backed off and continued to the water.

"Mum doesn't sound happy this morning. Cordie—"

"I know, I'll go check on her. You deal with Neevy's diaper."

"I think Neevy should go without a diaper," said Ione. "If

the seals can figure out where to do their business, so can she. Besides, we don't have many left."

"Whatever," I mumbled, not really listening. I was worried about how I was going to get my sisters and myself off this island. And I was worried about the seal. She looked weaker, with her eyes only halfway open. And I didn't want to scare Ione, but when the seal had barked at Henry, it didn't sound good and strong. It sounded just the opposite.

For her part, Ione was having the time of her life. She was playing house with a bunch of seals, and she believed her mum had returned and was lazing about on the beach, watching over her children, her nieces, and her nephews. The part of my plan that involved Ione seeing that the island had no selkies and giving up on the crazy story that I had started was failing splendidly.

"Good morning . . . uh . . . Mum," I said softly as I bent down next to the seal. "You don't look very good." She rolled over toward me as if to show me her wound, which was no better. "How did this happen to you?"

She looked at me with pain in her black eyes.

"Don't worry. I'll figure something out. Remember yesterday when you got up and swam and caught some fish? That made you feel better, didn't it?"

I rose and started down the beach. "Come on, Mum. Come on. Let's go get the fish!"

A shout from the cave interrupted my attempts to get the seal to the sea.

"Mum is not a dog, Cordie. You shouldn't treat her like one!"

I said something under my breath, something unkind, and the seal glared at me.

"Oh, don't even look at me like you understood that, Mum. You are just a seal. And you are not my mum, you know. I am just calling you that so Ione will stop bugging me. Now, I appreciate you getting us here and all, so why don't you be a good girl and go into the ocean and clean that thing off?" I pointed to the gaping cut on her shoulder.

But she just put her head down and gazed forlornly at the ocean.

This was not good.

I gathered some blackberry leaves, remembering how Mum would gather them from our yard, mash them up, and use them as a salve when we skinned our knees. Maybe, if I could place them on the seal's shoulder, it would give her a bit of ease.

A Daughter's Tale

There, there. That's better, right?

And if you are wondering if I think that the fact that there are blackberries here on the island and blackberries in our garden at home is a little coincidental, well the answer is yes. I do.

I can tell you that mashing the leaves up into a paste was not as easy as I thought it would be. Ione tried chewing them into a nice mash, but then her tongue got numb.

But I want to tell you things. Things while you sleep and maybe they will help you dream and maybe they will help you heal.

I am not sure which, but I would settle for either.

Once there were three sisters. One was older than the other two, much older. And then a sad thing happened. Well, before the sad thing, you should know that this family was very happy once. There was a mother with magical fingers who worked in a salon, and a father who repaired boats. They weren't rich, but the family was happy. And their three children were, too. Well, two of the children were. The last one was only a baby when the sad thing happened.

You see, their mother went away. And nobody knew where she went.

I bet you didn't know this, but when something bad like that happens to a kid, the other kids at school get all weird about it. None of them know what to say, so most of them don't say anything at all. It's like you have the plague. So all the friends the girls had kind of disappeared like fog does, so slightly at first that you don't notice, but then suddenly, it's just gone.

It made Ione angry and sad. She stopped even trying much at school. She'd never had an easy time with reading, but it got worse when her mum left.

And the baby, Neevy. She got strange fevers that came and went. And Da didn't think the oldest one knew how much it cost to go to a doctor. But she knew.

She knew that someone had to step forward and take care of everyone, so she did. Now, don't think that Da didn't do his part. He did. But he didn't make a lot of money, and the oldest daughter, well, she could tell that his heart was broken.

Maybe *shattered* is a better word. All the pieces were

probably there, but in such tiny bits that you couldn't even see how they might fit against each other again.

You can't put something that broken back together. You just can't.

So, slowly this family started to crumble, too.

But that oldest girl, well, she wasn't going to let this happen. She worked hard and got a job cleaning a store for a crusty old man. She didn't want to do it, but if that was what it took to make things better, then that was what she'd do.

I didn't tell you, yet, about the letter. The oldest girl found a note from her mum, stuffed in an old book about selkies. The letter made the girl feel better at first, because she could tell that her mum didn't really want to leave. Because you see, when people leave without saying goodbye, it's kind of hard to tell. The girl tried hard not to be mad at her mum. Very hard. But sometimes she couldn't help it. Mums shouldn't leave their children.

Even seals know that.

But here comes the bad part, because the girl made up a lie and told her sister that her mum was really a selkie and that was why she left.

Her sister believed her.

And here comes the weird part. See, the oldest girl does not believe her mum is a seal. It would be stupid and ridiculous if she did.

But she wants to. Really badly.

She wants to believe that inside of the seal, somewhere deep inside, is her mum. And if she could only find a way to reverse whatever magic caused her mum to turn into the seal in the first place, then she could finally fix it all.

She couldn't do it, though. Fix people. But maybe she could fix the other problem, the one with money. Folks know it's not polite to talk about money, especially not having any, but the girl was smart and figured out where to find a treasure. A treasure would make lots of things better. Maybe then Da wouldn't have to work as hard and then he could help the girls find their mum.

Someone else wants the treasure, though, and that would be an old lobster-face of a man named Mr. Doyle. But he's just a crazy old man. He believes Mum is a selkie, too. And I bet if someone asked him, he would say he believes the moon is a piece of goat cheese on a fine china plate that a selkie stole from him long ago and tossed up into the night sky as well.

That kind of crazy.

But not as crazy as when the seal showed up in Selkie Bay, convincing the sister that she was right. Mum was trapped in a sealskin.

So the oldest girl, she did something she probably shouldn't have. But it was brave and courageous. It was the kind of thing her mum would have done, she thought. She took the family boat and . . . well, you know the rest.

I left out the part where you got hurt. I don't know how it happened, but I am very sorry it did.

And I'm not sure why you stayed with us, or how you saved us, but I really want you to get better. Because I bet a lot of those little seals will miss you if you go away. They need you.

* * *

We need you, too.

The End of the Camp

I DREAMED I WAS IN A WHITE ROOM with wires and tubes and silent machines. There was a window with white curtains, the sheer kind that are almost useless because they don't keep any light out. They just make the light fuzzy. But under the fake drapes are blinds that can be pulled and when they are, all the light is blocked out.

But in my dream, they were open and the fuzzy light filled the room. It was a bedroom of sorts, for there were a couple of beds with white sheets. I thought there was someone in the bed, but before I could be sure, I woke up.

The seal, whom I had been napping next to, still slept soundly.

"You used to curl up next to Mum in her bed, just the same way, and I'd get in on the other side. Don't you remember, Cordie?"

I remembered.

I remembered the way Mum changed her breath so it

matched mine and how I could feel her heartbeat as I lay against her. And for just one minute, I let myself pretend that maybe I was there, snuggled next to Mum in her bed.

And it felt like home.

I put my arm around the seal and a little voice inside of me said, before I could catch it, *I miss you so much, Mum.*

"Don't cry, Cordie. Mum is looking better," Ione said bending down next to me. "Well, a little better, anyway."

"I wasn't crying," I said. "Just got some sand in my eyes. That's what I get for taking a nap on the beach." I hadn't meant to fall asleep so early in the day, but it was much easier to sleep on this strange little island during the light of day than in the black of night. I had never seen as many dark shadows as I had last night. But I had to get up now and figure out things—like a way to repair the boat, how to find some treasure, and what to do about that seal.

The sky, which had been a patchwork of white fog and beautiful blue just yesterday, was now the color of pavement this afternoon. Dark, gray, and menacing.

"I don't like the look of this," I said, standing up, dusting the sand from my bum, and pointing to the forming clouds.

"Well, I don't like the look of this," Ione said, holding the empty diaper bag upside down. The food, the bottled water, and the diapers were running out at about the same rate.

"I guess it is blackberries again," I said. Ione made a face. Some of the medium-sized seals brought fish to the beach, but I didn't have it in me to gut a fish, let alone build a fire and cook it up. And I didn't have a knife, either. But at least we could feed the fish to the large seal. Neevy, who was still snoring lightly in Ione's arms, was going to have to learn to like berries, and fast. Or raw fish.

"Maybe we ought to explore the island," I said. "We might find something else to eat. If blackberries grow here, maybe something else does, too."

"And we should decide where to start digging. I am sure there is lots of buried treasure here. Remember? If I were a selkie, I would definitely bury my treasures here. Do you think we should leave Mum?" Ione continued. "She might be worried about us if we aren't here when she wakes up."

"Well, why don't you wake her up and tell her, then?"

"Mum? Mum?" Ione said, kneeling next to the seal. She shook her a bit. "Mum, wake up."

But the seal didn't move.

"Cordie, Mum won't wake up."

I fell to my knees and felt the seal's chest to see if she was still breathing. She was, though they were light, small, slow breaths.

"She needs her rest, that's all."

"I don't like the way she's breathing. It's like she's not breathing at all."

I swallowed, feeling for the fib that would see me through

this one. "Seals, I mean selkies, can hold their breath for a long time, so don't worry. Let's just let her sleep."

I brushed my fingertips against her head. *Please be okay . . . Mum.*

I prayed the tide would come up and carry her out to sea while we were gone and that the sea would heal her.

And if the sea wasn't willing to make her well again, I hoped it would still take her so that at least she wouldn't have to die alone, beached on an old island. Maybe it would be better if we stayed with her, but I couldn't chance it. One look into Ione's eyes told me what she needed was hope. She'd already been abandoned by one mum. I didn't think she deserved to be left by two.

* * *

I gathered up Neevy as Ione said a proper good day to each of the selkie cousins, telling them that we were going to check out the rest of the island and asking them to keep an eye on Mum.

"Get her whatever she needs," she commanded.

Henry followed us as we trudged through the sand toward the caves.

"Go. Shoo," I said.

"Oogh," said Neevy.

"Don't shoo him, Cordie. He wants to come with us, can't you see? Come on, Henry." She bent down and he tried to jump into her arms, as if he was a puppy! He knocked her completely flat on her back, planting himself on her stomach.

"What? You've never seen a girl carry her cousin around?" She grunted.

I laughed and shook my head. Ione looked ridiculous. Laughing felt strange, seeing as we were nearly out of food, the sky was getting darker, and the air smelled like rain. And I was horribly worried about . . . Mum. Mum who left us months ago and Mum who lay injured on the beach. The two of them swirled around in my mind, coming together and floating apart until I didn't know what I really believed anymore. So I tried not to think about it. Instead, I let the laughter burble out, skipping happily past the angry box, which remained securely closed.

* * *

Past the three caves was another small opening.

"I wonder if we can fit through," Ione said, nudging Henry, who scampered on the ground in front of us. "Here, you try." She gave him another gentle poke with her foot.

Henry went inside the small opening. We waited.

"I am going to crawl in after him. Maybe that's where they keep the extra sealskins. You know, the ones for us." Ione sank to her hands and knees.

I pulled on the back of Ione's shirt, halting her progress

into the tunnel. "What if we are just people, Ione? What if, because Da's not a selkie, we aren't, either? I mean, don't you think if we were going to change into seals, we'd know it by now?" I spoke slowly, choosing words carefully. I didn't want to upset her, but I was one-thousand-percent sure there were no sealskins at the end of that tunnel.

Ione gave me a look like I was crazy and disappeared into the little cave without answering. I knew I shouldn't let her go and that I was being a very careless guardian, but I was tired and, well, sometimes a person just gets tired of always being in charge.

In a few seconds, Ione was backing out of the small cave. "Cordie, look at this!" She pulled out something dusty and brown and for a moment, the air got stuck in my throat. However, it was not a sealskin, but a worn leather bag with a rusted latch on the top. Henry dutifully followed her.

"It's like a tunnel in there, then it opens up. But look! I wonder what's in this."

As she unlatched the bag, I wondered something different. *Who put it there? And why?*

"Oh, biscuits! I love you!" Ione pulled a tin of biscuits from the bag to her lips and gave it a loud kiss. "I would marry you, biscuits!" She pried the lid off the familiar-looking tin. Seal Biscuits, the store in town. Of course. There were some chocolate biscuits and some that were just shortbread.

I don't think I'd ever seen Neevy so excited. She threw her arms about and made noises that were a cross between a snort and a squeal. I put a biscuit in her chubby hand and she gnawed on it happily.

I would not be lying if I said those biscuits were the best I'd ever had in my life, even if they were crumbly, stale, and tasted like old paper.

We munched happily as the wind whipped around our legs. I felt a sprinkle or two, but maybe that would be all there was of the rain. Sometimes winds brought heavy rains to Selkie Bay, and sometimes they petered out into nothing.

Neevy dropped some of her biscuit and Henry sniffed it, but didn't touch it. Ione swooped in, claiming the five-second rule, and gobbled it up. We were so distracted by the biscuits and the sputter of rain, we didn't even think about what else might be in the bag.

Our thoughts must have crossed in the air between us at the same time, for Ione handed me the tin and continued to search the bag. "Oh, look! There's a lighter! We can have a fire. And some packages of dried fruit, but they are brown and gross. Eww! I think this is a blanket, but it is very thin. And . . . hmm . . . what do you think a person would use this for, Cordie?"

Ione drew a long, ancient-looking spiked club from the depths of the bag.

The biscuit turned to sand in my mouth.

I knew whose bag it was.

And I had a pretty good guess why it was on the isle of the selkies.

The Puffer Fish Arrives

LITTLE HENRY WAS SQUIRMING AND BARKING, just as the wind picked up. I took the club from Ione and stuffed it back in the bag. "Don't ever touch this, Ione. Promise me. It's a bad thing."

She nodded, as Henry seemed further agitated.

"Something's got him riled. We should go and check on the others," she said, trying to hold him, but he wanted to get there on his own. He quickly scurried ahead. I gathered up Neevy and we ran to catch up. We overtook him in a few strides since running is faster than scuttling along.

The sky was becoming fiercely dark. The clouds swirled, large and puffy.

"The babies are all gone! Cordie, where are the babies?"

I surveyed the empty beach, searching for telltale bobbing heads in the waves. There were none.

"Well, probably Mum took them out to catch some dinner before the rain comes. That makes sense, doesn't it?"

I hoped it made sense.

I hoped she was okay.

And the babies, too. I hoped they were all okay.

"That's not what's supposed to happen. Remember the story? You should. You're the one who told it to me. The babies should be on the island during the storm so they don't get separated. Or scared."

Shaking my head noncommittally and shrugging at the same time, since I couldn't remember what I'd made up, I trudged down the beach to where we'd been using the *Dreaming Lass* as a windbreak. Another gust of wind came, blowing the sand and shells, releasing the money I'd set out to dry in a whirlwind of cash. "Ione, grab what you can!" I cried, but the money taunted and teased us, refusing to be caught.

I twirled around, Neevy in one arm, trying to catch a bill that floated just above my head with the other, when a gravelly voice chuckled and said, "Isn't that the way it is with Sullivans and money? Always chasing what they can't catch."

Mr. Doyle stood taller than I remembered, in black wading boots that went past his knees.

"What are you doing here?" I asked. "How did you get here? Where's your boat?"

"I might ask you the same," he said. "But I can see the *Dreaming Lass* sitting right there, such as it is. And my boat is past the rocks over there." He pointed to the large black rocks that were just to the north of the beach. He must have cut the motor before he got too close to the island or we'd have heard it.

"I see you've found my bag." He took a step closer and I was a little scared.

"I knew it was yours."

"So it would seem." He took another step closer and I saw *A Child's Book of Selkies* flapping in his hand. "And you've found some treasure, I see." He plucked a bill from the air.

"Give it back. It's not the island's treasure. It's our money. I brought it here."

"I don't believe it. Why would anyone bring money with them when they were hunting treasure? Most likely it's mine, buried here by my wife."

"Your wife, the *selkie*?" I said in a smart-mouth kind of way. I'd have been in trouble with Mum for using such a tone.

"Didn't I say as much?"

Ione walked over then, Henry in back of her, hiding behind her legs. "You said there was no island here, Mr. Doyle. You said the map was wrong. Why did you say the map was wrong if you'd already been here?"

"I lied."

It was then that he noticed Henry.

He gasped, dropping to his knees on the sand. "Saints preserve us," he said.

Ione stepped to the side so Henry was in full view.

A *Child's Book of Selkies* fell from the old man's fingertips and tumbled with a thud onto the sand. The jolt released the ancient pages from the tattered cover and they began to blow about in the wind and down to shore. Mr. Doyle was mumbling prayers or something, with his hands folded, but not closing his eyes like the folks did at Mass. He kept looking right at Henry.

And even though it was windy and cloudy and I could barely see it, I was pretty sure there was a tear rolling down his face.

Three seals came in from the water. I thought they were Betty, Charlie, and Oisin, but I couldn't be sure. They joined Henry, who had waddled in front of Ione, creating a barrier, silky and gray, between us and Mr. Doyle.

"Do you know what these are?" Mr. Doyle asked in a shaky voice.

"Selkies," said Ione with confidence. "Of course."

"No they aren't. They aren't selkies. Don't you know anything? They aren't selkies and they shouldn't be here." He was shaking his head.

"Of course they should. This is their island."

Ione had all the answers.

Mr. Doyle wiped his eyes and focused them again on Henry.

"No. These are pixie seals. And they shouldn't be here," he said for the second time.

"Why not, Mr. Doyle? Why shouldn't the pixie seals be here?" I fairly shouted to be heard over the wind, but even without it I'd have yelled, anyway. I didn't like that he'd showed up here. And I didn't like that he'd stolen my book. And I didn't like that he was crying.

"Because pixie seals are gone from here. Gone. I ought to know." He swallowed, then looked me in the eye hard, like he was daring me not to believe him. "I clubbed the last one years ago. Heaven help me." Mr. Doyle was sobbing now. "I clubbed the very last one."

Better Than Treasure

HE TOLD US ABOUT how he was forced by his father to do
horrible things. We sat in the large cave, hiding from the
wind. When I looked at Henry, Betty, Charlie, and Oisin,
I hated Mr. Doyle. But when I looked at Mr. Doyle himself,
crying like a baby, I couldn't hate him as much.

Maybe sometimes we all do things we later wish we
hadn't.

Ione was less forgiving.

"I can't believe you clubbed baby seals," she said, her eyes
so black and dark and full of venom I would have thought
she was putting a curse on him.

"It was a different time," he said.

Ione snorted and continued to pet Henry, whose head
was lying in her lap. Neevy was sleeping, too, in my lap.
And Mr. Doyle sat across from us, never taking his eyes
from the three seals that separated us.

"And when the seals were gone, my father thought he'd

won. Even the fact that his leg—which he broke running away from the black seal—had healed poorly could not diminish his victory. He'd kept the seals away from the bay. But alas, the fishing was never very good again."

I remembered the story he'd told me in his shop and I thought about my da's research project, searching for the missing pixie seals. He thought the boat traffic had driven the seals away. Instead, the poor things had been hunted and slaughtered.

And yet, here they were.

"And the nightmares never ceased," Mr. Doyle continued. "I did lots of wishing, praying, and crying into the sea, hoping to bring back what I'd killed." He glanced up at me, then down again. "Things don't always come back just because we want them to."

He told us then about his wife, Pegeen, and how she'd had the look of the selkies his father had warned him about, but he couldn't keep himself away from her. And how, almost thirteen years to the day that they'd met, she vanished with all of his money.

Thirteen years.

"I can see you're doing the math, Cordelia. Yes, your mum lived in Selkie Bay for exactly thirteen years before she left."

"Doesn't prove anything," I said quietly.

A few more of the seals had swum up and now were huddled near the entrance of the cave. But the black one wasn't there. A sick knot formed in my stomach.

"It is the strangest thing, all of these seals. It's like seeing ghosts." He reached out to touch one, Betty, but she barked at him and he quickly withdrew his hand. "Real enough, I suppose."

We were quiet then; the only noise was the whistling of the wind outside.

"Why did you steal our book? And how?" Ione asked, breaking the stillness of the cave.

"You were too busy looking for that seal at the dock and lying about not going anywhere that you didn't even notice. And I needed to see the map again. I might have known where the island was, but not the treasure. I've searched before." He pointed to his brown bag. "But not for years. There was never a trace of a treasure or a seal. Not a trace."

"Why did you have a club, then? Were you planning to use it?"

Mr. Doyle looked shocked. "Oh no! Never again in all my days would I use such a thing. I brought it here . . . because I couldn't stand the sight of it. Because . . . when it sat in my closet at home, I could still hear the cries of the seal mums as we . . ."

Mr. Doyle didn't finish. I don't think either Ione or I wanted him to.

"And did the book tell you where the treasure was?" I asked, changing the subject.

He looked at the silver silken creatures around us. "No. You yourself know the book doesn't reveal the true secrets of the island." He put out his hand again, this time palm up, and placed it under Betty's nose. She sniffed it, then nuzzled his hand. He petted her head and almost smiled through a new crop of tears. "But maybe some things are worth more than treasure."

Porridge Is Boring

MR. DOYLE WAS STILL SNIFFLING when he said he needed to go check on his boat, so I wrapped Neevy in a cozy blanket rescued from the bottom of the bag, plunked her in a drowsy Ione's lap, and followed him. Maybe he wanted to have a good cry in peace. Maybe he thought it would make him feel better. I knew it wouldn't, though. I cried enough when Mum first left I could have written a book on crying, bigger and thicker than any selkie book. It never made me feel any better. Not one bit.

The raindrops were tiny, but there were so many of them, like a curtain of rain.

"Where is it?" I asked.

"My boat? Behind those rocks." He pulled out a crumpled handkerchief, blew his nose loudly, then pointed to some rocks not too far past the beach.

"I don't see it."

"It's there. Probably just hidden." He waded out in his long boots, into the swirling foam.

"Are you sure?" I asked.

"Course I am sure. I know where I anchored my own boat," he grumbled over his shoulder, still going toward the rocks.

"Well, if your boat is over there, whose boat do you suppose *that* is?" For there, riding on the waves far to the right of where Mr. Doyle was walking, was an old polluter of a boat, drifting farther and farther away, off into the sunset like the end of an old movie.

I could have sworn I saw six or seven little silver heads following in its wake, as if to see it off.

I thought he'd be mad, but he just mumbled, "Well, good riddance to you, you rusted-out pail of barnacles!" He caught me watching him and muttered, "What are you looking at?"

I shrugged.

Mr. Doyle was perplexing. He'd just lost his boat and he seemed not to care! Instead, he walked slowly, gently, back to the cave and over to the seals, where he sat among them. He began petting them and saying kind things. And they let him.

Except for the black seal.

She had not yet returned from the sea.

* * *

It was getting too late in the day to do anything about our boat situation, not to mention the fact that it was still rainy.

So Mr. Doyle built us a small fire in the cave and we began what was sure to be a very long night.

"How did the three of you find your way here?" he asked us as we warmed ourselves. We didn't have much wood, so we burned the old club. As the flames flickered, Mr. Doyle let out a sigh. Ione and I did, too. That club was something that none of us ever wanted to see again.

"She led us here. Mum, I mean," Ione said. "It's okay, Cordie. Remember, he already knows."

When Mr. Doyle grudgingly produced a small tin of fresh Seal Biscuits in a much more modern tin, Ione decided she could forgive him for his past deeds, as long as they were never repeated.

"She? The black seal? Led you here?" he asked in a broken-up way in between biscuit bites.

Ione nodded. "But she's not a seal. She's a selkie." Mr. Doyle glanced at me and I looked away. It certainly had seemed like the seal had led us here, or maybe pushed us here. Either way, we'd never have made it without her.

"I'm worried about her, Cordie," Ione said.

"She's fine."

But if she was fine, why didn't she come back?

This was the second mum I had asked such a question about.

Ione looked toward the opening of the cave forlornly. "Where is she?"

I wanted to distract Ione from worrying about the seal,

and to distract myself, too. But I didn't have it in me to make up another selkie tale. "Let's talk about something else."

"How about we talk about porridge," said Ione after a few moments of awkwardness. "Like in the story of the three bears. I have always wondered if it is just the same thing as oatmeal. If it is, why don't they just call it oatmeal?"

"I don't know," I said.

Ione waited for Mr. Doyle to answer her question, but he didn't.

"I guess porridge is kind of boring," Ione said.

With that, we sat gazing into the flames. Silence hung in the air like mist, so thick you could almost see it. Or smell it. The silence smelled like seaweed and mint and smoke.

Then Mr. Doyle's scratchy voice, low and deep, began to echo softly through the cave.

A Tale Not About Selkies

There is a tale my father told me once, about a time before the selkies came. There have always been folks who were closer to the sea than others. Folks who hear the call of the sea and feel it thump deep in their chest with each beat of their own heart. The waves rise and fall in time with their own breathing. They say that inside every man and woman is an ocean of sorts. For some, it's more real than for others.

So, in the time before selkies, there was a kingdom and in this kingdom were two sons, Lorcas and Seamus. Lorcas was fine and strong and a treasure to his parents. Seamus, well, he was dark haired and dark eyed, with more sea in his veins than blood. Seamus was the wild one who stayed not on the path his parents had chosen for him. Little did his parents know that you cannot control a river. It must always make its own way, even if its path is ne'er the straightest one. Nor the easiest.

Lorcas and Seamus were devoted to each other, as good brothers are. But a terrible accident befell Lorcas and he lost his sight. The future his parents had planned for him withered and eventually blew away with the wind. He sat in his home, doing nothing, thinking nothing, being nothing.

But the same wind that carried away Lorcas's future deposited it at the feet of Seamus. He would now be the favored son, if he chose. He no longer had to cut paths through harshness to make his way. The easy life could be his.

Seamus, however, with the ocean in his veins, simply went to his brother and told him, "Lorcas, I shall be your eyes now." And whether it was magic or love at work, it didn't matter, for from that moment on, everything Seamus saw, Lorcas could see, too. It was as if the oceans inside of both of them became one sea. One sea.

In the Wee Hours

IONE AND HENRY WERE SNORING SOFTLY and the rest of the seals were, too. Even Neevy had been put to sleep by the spell Mr. Doyle's tale cast.

I had started to doze myself, when the abrupt end of the story roused me.

"It just ends there?"

He nodded.

"What does it mean?" I asked.

"A story means whatever you need it to mean."

I was going to ask, *What does that even mean?* But then I imagined him saying, *Whatever you need it to mean,* and I would have felt the need to throw a shoe at him, so I didn't.

"Sometimes, Cordelia, we do things for others, for our family, that might not be the things we want to, but out of love, we do them. That's what I think the story of Lorcas and Seamus is about. Doing what you must for your family."

"Do you have any family now?"

He didn't answer at first, but turned his attention to the opening of the cave. "Rain's tapering off and there's work to do," he said gruffly, then rose and made sure the fire was truly out, without looking at any of us.

I shouldn't have asked. Neevy snorted a little in her sleep and I put a calming hand on her bald head. To the other side of me, Ione rearranged herself and I reached out and smoothed her hair. I thought about how lucky I was to have them and a lump rose in my throat. I would do anything for them. Anything.

"Well, look who's here," said Mr. Doyle as the black seal slowly hauled herself inside the cave, then lay down, breathing heavily.

"*Mum!*" I extracted myself from my sleeping sisters and rushed over to her. Her large eyes were closed and her skin felt saggy, not smooth and tight like it had yesterday. And when she rolled over to show me her side, my breath caught in my throat.

The gash was worse than ever.

Mr. Doyle made no move to come closer.

"Can you help me? I don't know what to do for her," I begged.

He opened his mouth to say something, then closed it again, shaking his head. I saw him scoot a bit away from the fire, away from us.

"You can't possibly be afraid of her," I said, all the while stroking Mum's fur. "She needs help."

"I promised myself after Pegeen I'd have nothing to do with real and true selkies. Nothing," he whispered. He had squashed himself up against the side of the cave, as far from us as possible. I was pretty certain he was trembling.

I was, too. But not from fear.

"Nothing except trying to make your living off of them!" I cried. "I haven't forgotten what you did to Ione—parading her around on your stupid boat. Filling her head with stories about—"

I stopped. I'd done my share of filling Ione's head with stories. I'd even let my own head fill up with stories of treasure.

And look where that had led me.

"If you'll keep that"—he pointed at Mum—"*her* there, I'll slip outside and start repairing your boat. It's our only way off this island and someone has to do it. We should leave at dawn."

"I'll hold her, but she's too weak to attack you, if that's what you're worried about," I said, wrapping my arms loosely around her.

Mr. Doyle crept by, but as he passed Mum's head, her black eyes opened and she looked right at him. He moved quickly then, like he'd stepped on a flame.

Mum never had liked Mr. Doyle much.

175

* * *

By morning, Mr. Doyle had finished patching the hole in the *Dreaming Lass*, using tools from his brown bag.

"Seems clear enough, but we need to get out soon. I don't want to be racing that storm." He pointed over to some dark clouds to the north. "Can't tell how fast it's coming," he said. "Your da is probably having fits. First your mother and now—"

He didn't need to finish.

"You never called the authorities." It was not a question.

"Of course not. What kind of man do you think I am?"

That was a question I could not answer. What kind of man *was* Archibald Doyle? Was he the mean, miserly man who Ione hated just because of the look of him? Was he the strange, gentle man who gave a sad little girl who missed her mum a nice day out on his boat? Was he the exploiter, ready to use a child to increase his business? Was he the crusty yet repentant man who now sat feeding fish to the gray pixie seals he had once caused to vanish?

Or was he somehow a mixture of all these?

I would probably never understand him. Even now, as I tried to put the puzzle of Mr. Doyle together in my head, I was left with a piece that didn't fit at all. The piece of him that feared Mum.

Mum slept. I placed a sleeping Neevy beside her because she had seemed to like it when Ione had done that. Ione was brushing Mum's fur with her fingertips, singing to her. I couldn't tell if she was running a fever or not, because who knew how hot a seal was supposed to be.

"She looks better, don't you think, Cordie?"

"Yes, she does," I lied. She didn't look better at all. I sat down next to her and examined the wound again. I was pretty sure it was from the propeller, and that it was infected. She'd gotten hurt while helping us.

Of the pixie seals, only Henry stayed with us in the cave. Some were out with Mr. Doyle, and some weren't here at all, probably out frolicking in the waves.

"Are we really going to leave without finding the treasure?" Ione whispered. "We came all this way and we didn't even dig once."

I didn't care about the treasure anymore. Gold, silver, money. None of it would help the black seal right now. "Mr. Doyle has been coming here for years, Ione. Don't you think if Grace O'Malley's pirate treasure was here, he would have found it?"

"Pirates are smart and selkies are smarter. And I bet Mum knows where that pirate treasure is. Too bad she can't change herself back to a person and tell us. Hey, Cordie, when do you think she'll be able to change back?"

"I don't know."

"I bet it said in the book. I wish Mr. Doyle hadn't let it rip apart and blow away into the ocean."

Ione kept talking, but the only words I heard were, *When*

do you think she'll be able to change back? ringing through my brain, again and again. I laid my head against Mum's side and felt the beat of her heart, soft and warm, against my ear.

Mr. Doyle barely set one foot into the cave. "Cordelia, get your sisters. We need to leave." Then he turned his back and returned to the beach.

Mr. Doyle was right. I knew he was right. I could hear the thick patter of the rain starting up again. The drops were getting bigger. If we didn't go soon, we might not have another chance today.

But I couldn't make myself get up from beside the seal— from beside Mum. I couldn't make myself leave my mum. I was holding her, not tightly, because I didn't want to hurt her, but with strong arms, as if that could somehow make her strong again.

"Cordie, you need to come. Now." But it wasn't Mr. Doyle's gruff voice that traveled the distance from the cave opening to my ear. It was a voice both broken and smooth at the same time.

It was Da.

The Pinniped

DA'S TINY RESEARCH BOAT, the *Pinniped*, was anchored in the small lagoon of the Kingdom of the Selkies. I could see it from the mouth of the cave, just past where Mr. Doyle stood, bent over the *Dreaming Lass*. I'd only heard about the *Pinniped*, never seen it myself except in pictures, but I knew, with its bright yellow hull, that it had to be the old boat.

"I thought it was rusty and ruined," was the first thing I said to Da. Not *I missed you* or *I am sorry.*

But then he was hugging me and I was standing, hugging him back, and Ione and a sleeping Neevy were all gathered in there, too.

"That's the boat I went to repair. In Glenbay. I didn't want to tell you in case I couldn't do it." He was kissing our heads and nearly crushing us, but we didn't care. He hadn't yelled at us for being here, or told us how mad he was. That would come later.

If there was anything I was certain of, it was that at some point, my father would have words for me.

"We need to go, girls. Before the storm hits," he said.

"So it's finally coming then. Moving faster than I thought," Mr. Doyle interjected. Apparently he'd given us enough of a private reunion. "Got here as fast as I could, you know, when I saw they'd gone. But there was a thing that happened with my boat making it rather difficult to leave . . ."

"If I hadn't run into Raj Patel, I wouldn't have known where the lot of you were, now, would I?" Da looked at me as he said it. "And yes, Archibald. The storm is coming. Some say it's the storm of the century."

"Storm of the century. That rhymes," said Ione.

"No it doesn't. The words just sound the same at the beginning," I said.

"That's what I meant."

"Seriously, girls. We'll have plenty of time to talk later. And believe me, there is plenty to talk about," Da said.

I knew that last comment was for me, but I didn't want to think about it. Not yet, anyway.

"Cordie, is that a seal right behind you?" Da said, noticing Mum for the first time.

"It's Mum," said Ione, kneeling down beside her. "And this is Henry." She pointed to the other side of her, where Henry, alert like a little pup, regarded us all.

Da stared at Henry for a long moment, then shook his head in disbelief. "A pixie seal. And I thought I was imagining things out there," he muttered. Then he looked at Mum.

"You call this big, black seal *Mum?*"

"That's because it is Mum. She's a selkie," Ione said.

Da looked at me to translate. But I just couldn't find the words. Neevy awoke with a cry. Henry barked.

And then the wind began keening.

"We don't have much time if we are going to get out of here in one piece!" Da called over the howls of the wind.

"We are not leaving Mum behind," Ione cried.

"Ione, come *on!*" Da yelled. He was holding Neevy and making his way to where Mr. Doyle stood with the *Dreaming Lass.* "Archibald, tie the *Lass* to the *Pinniped* with the towline. We'll pull her behind us."

"Aye, Captain," Mr. Doyle said, saluting Da in an almost comical way.

"Cordie, get Ione away from that seal. We need to get out of here. The island won't be safe for very much longer."

"I am not leaving her," said Ione, holding on to the seal. "It's Mum! She's a selkie! Cordie knows it's true. She told me all about the selkies!"

The whistling and shrieking through the cracks and crevices of the cave was becoming unbearable.

"Ione, that seal is not your mother. If Cordie said so, then Cordie . . . well, she made it up and she should know better," Da yelled, over the bluster of it all. *"Tell her, Cordie! Tell her the truth!"*

But I couldn't tell Ione the truth because I didn't know what the truth was anymore.

"Ione. I am your father. I am not lying to you. That is not your mum. Get in the boat. *Now!*"

I'd never heard Da use a tone like that. Ione hadn't, either. Stunned, she got up from Mum and walked over to Da.

"But Cordie told me. Cordie said—" she whispered, but she stopped. She could tell by looking at him that he wasn't lying.

There was a loud crack. I think it was my heart, as Ione walked by with the worst expression of pain I'd ever seen on anybody's face. *"How could you, Cordie? How could you lie to me? Why?"*

And again I had no answers because I could not find even a single word to explain anything. Because sometimes there are no explanations. There are only moments, one after the next, when you know what you have to do.

I knelt back down to the seal and held on to her.

When Da came back for me, after taking Ione and Neevy to the boat, I was still there.

"Cordie, we'll sort this all out later. Come," he said.

And then there was a word. Just one word my lips formed, and it was out of my mouth before I could stop it.

"*No.*"

The Tale I Wanted to Tell Da

There was a girl who stopped believing in anything. In everything.

And then, for some reason, she started again. And what she can't tell you is that this seal is really . . . is really her mum. And she can't tell you because if she says it out loud and it sounds stupid, it will break the magic and her mum will be gone forever.

So it is a short story of words that will never be spoken.

Because the girl has no words left.

Over the Edge

IT TOOK THE THREE OF US, Da, Mr. Doyle, and me, to get Mum on the boat. And it took a lot of convincing on Da's part to get Mr. Doyle to even help at all.

"Archibald Doyle, stop being an eejit and lend a hand for crying out loud!" Da had finally yelled. Mr. Doyle crossed himself twice before holding Mum's tail so Da and I could guide the heavier part of Mum onto the *Dreaming Lass*. Then we had to transfer her to the *Pinniped*.

The storm was now descending upon us in full force.

The old Cordie would have already thrown up twice with all the rocking, between the small boat and the small research vessel, but all I could think about was the seal.

Mum.

I wasn't sure what changed Da's mind about the whole thing, for since that one word, *no*, I hadn't uttered anything.

Once Mum was on board and we had our life vests on,

Da and Mr. Doyle secured the *Dreaming Lass*. The *Pinniped's* motor rumbled and Da steered the boat away from the Kingdom of the Selkies.

I held Mum and Ione held Neevy as we left behind all thoughts of gold and treasure.

The waves beat against the side of the boat and then the *Pinniped* jerked to a stop. Da revved the motor, but we went nowhere.

"What happened?" Mr. Doyle called over the sound of the storm.

"I'm not sure. We're stuck maybe." Da looked over the edge of the boat, then behind, to where the *Dreaming Lass* floated.

A large wave came and shoved us all to the side, nearly smashing the *Pinniped* against the two guardian rocks that protected the island.

"I can't get her loose!" Mr. Doyle cried, and another wave pounded us.

Da's eyes widened and his voice shook when he spoke. "I've got to get us untangled somehow. It's the towline between the *Lass* and the *Pinniped*," he said to Mr. Doyle, and he threw one trembling leg over the side of the boat.

Mr. Doyle grabbed my da by the shirt and pulled him back. "Don't you dare go over the side. The whole town knows your lack of swimming skill. You almost drowned once. And it's bad enough with their mother gone! Those girls need you!" He looked ready to slug my da in the face, but Da shouted right back at him.

"If I don't get us loose, it won't matter! We'll all be smashed against the rocks!" He jerked himself away from Mr. Doyle.

"Don't do it, Da! Don't!" cried Ione, sobbing and reaching out a hand to him, as if that would stop him.

I wanted to cry out, too. But my voice held nothing. Instead I looked down at Mum and she was looking at me. Her dark eyes spoke to me in a way that words never could. Then she waggled her seal body away from me.

No.

My lips couldn't move and as the giant wave came and swept over the side of the *Pinniped*, Da ran over and grabbed on to me. Huge buckets of water splashed over us, beating us down onto the small, splintery deck.

When the wave retreated, the seal was no longer there.

"Mum!" Ione cried. Mr. Doyle was holding on to her and Neevy, and Da had me.

"Brace yourselves, girls. This next one is going to be even bigger!" Mr. Doyle called out.

We huddled down, but then instead of the next wave crashing upon us, we rose up on it, past the guardian rocks, into the open blue.

"We're unstuck!" Mr. Doyle cried. And sure enough, we flew over the next wave. Whatever had tangled the towline below the surface and paralyzed the *Pinniped* had suddenly, miraculously become untangled.

Da raced to the controls and soon we were speeding out of danger, back toward the town of Selkie Bay, with the *Dreaming Lass* bouncing behind us.

Ione snuggled up next to me. She gave me Neevy and I held her tight.

"It was Mum that saved us," Ione said. "I saw her go over the side and then we were free. It was her. And now she's gone again."

All I could do was look behind us, as the Kingdom of the Selkies disappeared into the clouds and mist. And there was nothing to say, because Ione had said it all.

* * *

In about an hour, we had gone through the worst of the storm and were nearing the harbor. We were wet through and through. I understood now why Neevy cried to have her diaper changed.

"I didn't even get to say goodbye to Henry," Ione sulked. "Or Betty, or Daisy, or Diana, or Charlie, or Oisin, or . . . oh, Cordie, I knew I would forget their names."

William, Kate, Brian, Finn, Sorcha, Fergal, Mo, Dearbla, and Michael.

"The seals?" Da asked. "You named them all?"

"Of course. They needed names. And they are selkies."

"No, Ione, they are not. They are pixie seals, the same species my team tried to find years ago. They'd all but vanished from these parts."

I looked over at Mr. Doyle, but he was busy driving the boat. I wondered if he felt bad that his own boat was gone, or if he was like Da, just glad to be alive.

"But now," Da continued, "these seals have made a comeback—probably breeding out on that island all these years. Why, I couldn't believe what I was seeing in the water. I'd have never found that island myself if I hadn't followed them. Their little silver heads bobbing along led me right to you."

"Why didn't Mum look like the rest of them?"

"The big black seal wasn't one of them. She was a different kind of seal altogether. Perhaps a gray seal, but she was unusually dark in color. I'll show you in my book when we get home."

Ione didn't argue with Da, but when she looked over at me, I knew she no longer thought I was a liar. We knew the black seal had saved us all.

And we knew it was just what Mum would have done.

Words

"CORDIE, YOU HAVEN'T SPOKEN in two days and I'm tired of it." Da looked up at me from his bowl of oatmeal and tossed his spoon on the table. "You haven't said a word since you were on that island."

I wanted to so badly. I wanted to say something.

Anything.

Not that there was much I could have said.

Ione had explained to Da everything that had happened. And Da had explained to me exactly how crazy and irresponsible it had been to take my sisters out on the *Dreaming Lass* to find a hidden island.

He was right. It had been irresponsible. And probably stupid. If I still had an angry box, I am sure it would be open and I'd be raging at myself for being such an idiot.

But the box was empty. Gone.

"I'm done with this," Da said. Then he stood and picked up the phone. "I should have done this a long time ago," he said. As he dialed, he pointed to Ione and me. "Get ready, and Neevy, too. We are going out."

* * *

Our car was old and rusty, like the *Pinniped*, but at least it wasn't yellow.

It took us an hour and a half to get to the city.

Ione blabbed the whole way, asking Da questions about where we were going and why we were going there, but Da was mostly quiet about it all. Ione didn't seem afraid to leave the house like she had before. Instead, she was a chatterbox.

Neevy, lucky Neevy, slept the whole way there.

As for me, I just leaned my head against the window and stared. I didn't see anything but a blur. And I didn't think of anything except for the black seal I'd come to think of as Mum. Even though now, not being in the Kingdom of the Selkies, it was hard to think about Mum being that seal, hard to imagine.

But hard to let go of, just the same.

"We are here," Da said as he pulled up to the City Hospital. "She's here."

He quietly led us up to the fourth floor, down a white corridor, and into a waiting room painted a soft blue. At a counter, a nurse looked up.

"Hello, Mr. Sullivan," she said.

Da smiled, then motioned for us to sit on a couch, so we did.

"Stay here for a minute," he said, and he disappeared down the hall into a room.

"Why do you suppose we are here?" Ione whispered. She might not have had much in the way of manners, but Ione knew to use a quiet voice in a hospital.

I shrugged. She should have known I wouldn't answer. Or that I couldn't.

"Cordie, you first," Da said, standing in the doorway and motioning for me to come. He stopped me as I was about to step inside. "She made me promise, Cordie. And that's why I was holding on to the money, in case I needed it for the . . . treatments. But I never should have agreed to it. I never should have."

The room was white, all white, with wires and tubes and silent machines. There was a window with white curtains, the sheer kind that are almost useless because they don't keep any light out. And there were two beds. The one by the door was empty, but the one by the window had someone in it.

She didn't look like I remembered. Her dark hair was gone. She saw me staring at her head. "I guess I look like Neevy. We could be twins."

And her voice didn't sound quite the same. It was quieter. And when I got close enough, she didn't smell like she was supposed to, either. Not like seaweed and mint. She smelled like chemicals.

"Cordie, I know this is hard, so please, just listen," she said. "I am getting better now, but at first, I was so afraid. I felt I had to fight this battle on my own. I didn't want you to see me so weak. I didn't want you to remember me . . . like this. Maybe I was wrong. Your da thinks it was a mistake to have kept it from you."

Her big dark eyes were watery.

"But I missed you, Cordie, I missed you so much." She held out her hand to me, pale and thin with little webs between her fingers, and I took it in my own. I could feel her heart beating, there in her hand.

So I reached up and put my arms around her and hugged her. And then she was crying and telling me things I couldn't quite hear, mumbly things against my hair. But I didn't care what she said, just that she was there, next to me, my heart trying to find the rhythm of hers.

Da brought Ione in then. She nearly climbed over me to get to Mum. She gasped at the baldness, but recovered quickly. "I can give you some of my hair," she said, reaching up to touch the fuzz on the top of Mum's head that was so like our baby sister's. "Cordie says I have too much, anyway." Then Ione whispered to me, "If you have to get bald to have a sealskin, I don't think I want one."

Da placed Neevy in Mum's arms and then she truly cried,

the large kind of tears a person cries when they've been holding on to them forever.

"I missed you girls so much." She sobbed for a long time, then she pulled out of the hug and looked at us queerly. "But I would see you sometimes, in my dreams at night. I saw you out on the *Dreaming Lass*, just the three of you, and I knew it was a dream, for my girls would never do anything so foolish. And I saw you, surrounded by seals, small gray ones. And I saw you in a storm, a terrible storm, and I was worried." She reached up and rubbed her shoulder, her left one, then went back to rocking Neevy in her arms. "I can't explain it because it sounds so strange, but I felt close to you . . . somehow . . ."

Her voice trailed off.

I could feel Da's gaze upon me and so I turned to face him. He was shaking his head. "I didn't tell her a thing," he whispered to me. "Not a thing."

And my tears came then, and the words too—finally, the words came.

"I love you, Mum."

Things You Can Explain

MUM CAME HOME A FEW WEEKS LATER, just as Da was
starting his new job as a scientist again, studying the return
of the pixie seals to Selkie Bay. He was awarded something
called a "nice fat grant" to continue the research he started
thirteen years ago, but supposedly now it is even more remarkable. A species that somehow escaped from extinction
can teach us all, Da said.

School would be starting soon, right after tourist season,
and though Mum was far too weak to return to Maura's
salon, Ione and I swept the hair from the floor to make a
little extra spending money. Most was spent at Seal Biscuits, but I also went to Whale of a Tale and placed an
order for a used copy of *A Child's Book of Selkies*. The book-
seller told me it would be hard to find and that I might
have to wait, but I didn't care. I thought it would be nice to
have around.

Ione asked almost every day to go on the boat with Da so

she could have a chance at spotting Henry or Betty, or the rest of them. And if Da said no, then she'd hit up Mr. Doyle. Da had given him the use of the *Dreaming Lass* for a while, as repayment for watching over us on the island. Of course, Mr. Doyle hadn't wanted to accept the help, coming from the Sullivans and all, and made lots of grumbling grunts about it. He was still prickly around Mum. But since Mum didn't want to owe Archibald Doyle anything, Da eventually convinced him of the fairness of it. Da liked paying his debts. And it turned out better than Mr. Doyle could have imagined. Lots of folks wanted to see the return of the pixie seals from a cute little boat with an environmentally friendly tiny outboard motor rather than from the bow of a big, nasty, old polluter.

The day my book came in, I raced to Whale of a Tale and back, resisting the lure of the familiar bench. When I got home, out of breath from the run, I sat on the floor next to Mum as she rocked Neevy, trying to get her to nap, although I think Mum was losing that battle. Neevy was no longer the napper she'd been before Mum left. Ione was lying on her stomach, building a book castle for the chess pieces again. Quietly, I thumbed through the old pages.

Somewhere between Fantasy and Reality,
between Myth and Legend
lies the Kingdom of the Selkies.

And I thought about how some things can be explained, like how an almost-extinct species of seals can find a way, on a secret island, to save themselves and come back stronger. And about how some things can't be explained, like how a mum battling a deadly illness can be in a hospital bed, miles away, but also on a mist-covered island, watching over her daughters through the eyes of a seal, at the exact same time.

"What are you reading, Cordie?" Mum asked. When I held up the book, a tear spilled out from Mum's eye, trailing perfect and silver down her cheek.

"So what do you think? Do you believe in creatures that can shed their sealskins and shift into people?" I asked her softly as she wiped her eyes.

"I believe in many things, Cordie. But most of all, I believe in you."

Author's Note

The pixie seals of Selkie Bay are fictional—like Selkie Bay itself. I based them on a recent incident involving the discovery of a hidden monk seal habitat in the Mediterranean Sea, which allows monk seals to reproduce and repopulate unhindered by humankind. Currently, monk seals are the most endangered seal species in the world. A similar situation befell a population of gray seals of the British Isles, wherein secret breeding locations helped to sustain, and even increase, their dwindling numbers. Although rare in some places, the gray seal is now not officially on the endangered list. However, seals, like all marine animals, are at risk due to the mistreatment of the ocean and the disappearance of appropriate habitats in which seal mothers can give birth to their pups.

The comeback of the gray seal is not the only example of a species finding a way to save itself. In another instance, the Guadalupe seal was thought to have been hunted into extinction in 1892, only to be rediscovered in the 1950s, hiding out on a secret island.

Seals and humans share a troubled past. I wish I could report that the brutality of seal clubbing is ancient history, but there are still countries in the world that condone this outdated and cruel practice. Culling refers to the act of decreasing one population in order to increase another. Some governments allow the seal population to be culled in order to increase fish populations. More fish equals more profit. And in some places seals, like the lovely baby harp seals called "white coats," are still hunted for their pelts.

As for the legend of the selkie, the mythology surrounding creatures that can change shape from seal to human has been around for many centuries. I am only adding one more humble tale to a larger collection of things you can explain, and things you can't.

Acknowledgments

Thanks to Jo Volpe and Wesley Adams for nurturing this tiny seed of an idea into a full-grown book. For that's all it was at first—just Cordie and her missing mum and the legends of the selkies, and not much else. Jo always believed the story would eventually bloom and Wes gave it the space to grow. For that I will always be grateful.

And big shout-outs to everyone who kept my ship from

sinking as I sailed my boat into that mist between legend and truth. My greatest thanks to you all:

Nancy Villalobos and Chris Kopp
The students and staff of Jefferson Elementary School
Holly Pence and Kathy Duddy
Danielle Barthel and Jaida Temperly
The whole FSG TEAM (you rock!)
Gilbert Ford (for the lovely cover!)
John III, Tammi, John IV, Hope, and Jacob Moore
Susan, Jim, Elora, and Mia Daniels
My parents, John and Nancy Moore
And my amazing husband, Sean

Of course, there would be no book without my daughters, whose lives I raided. I have always wanted to write about sisters. My girls, you are the reason there are words on the page. You are the reason there are stories to write.